Crown Deception

Crown Deception

Howard Lufburrow

Acknowledgements

Crown Deception has been a labor of love for the last 5 years. I want to thank my staff members that have supported me in my profession as a dentist. Without their support I would not have had the time to work on this book.

I want to thank everyone that has helped with proofreading and editing, while giving me encouragement to finish the book.

And especially my family for all they have done to help with this book. Especially important were our visits to The Netherlands while my son Blake was in school there. During our trips to Leiden, I began to imagine some of the characters and scenes in the book.

Most importantly I want to thank my wife, Debbie for her love and support while I worked to finish the book.

Chapter 1
Triumph County Morgue

After Jake Patterson parked his car outside the morgue at the county hospital, he sat for a few minutes to gather strength to go inside. He hated looking at dead bodies.

As he approached the morgue's glass doors, he could see Paul Baker, Chief of Police of Triumph, Texas, waiting. About a year earlier Paul had talked him into helping with difficult homicide cases that required some dental expertise. Now, here he is again. Not the way Jake wanted to spend a Saturday evening.

He ignored Paul's outstretched hand. "I told you last time, never again. You know how much I hate this. I wish I'd never told you I took those classes in Forensic Dentistry. I didn't become a dentist to hang out in morgues." Bad memories flooded his mind as he anticipated the formaldehyde smell and the cold feel of the morgue. Memories from anatomy class in dental school were mixed with the painful memories of the tragic loss of his wife and parents years earlier.

"Jake, I really appreciate this and I think you might just find it interesting. Come on, let's go on into the autopsy room. Mack's waiting. He wants your opinion on something."

Dr. Mack Turner, the only pathologist and coroner in Triumph for the last four years, had brought a new level of Forensic medicine not usually seen in a small town. Although Jake hated his few experiences in the morgue, he had to admit that every encounter with Mack taught him something new about his own profession.

As they entered the prep room, Mack waved them over to where a young deceased male laid uncovered on the autopsy table. Without even a "hello," he launched into the case. "Gentlemen, we have here a 25 to 30 year old male, six foot three inches in height, weight, 198 pounds, and no identification present. It appears his death is due to some sort of overdose. I'm waiting on the toxicology report but it won't be here until sometime tomorrow."

Paul Baker interrupted. "Mack, let's get to the point of why you asked me to call Jake in to help out."

"Oh, sorry Chief, I get carried away sometimes. Jake, you're going to love this," he exclaimed excitedly. "Over here."

Jake and Paul walked near to the body and leaned in as Mack directed him to the maxillary right side of the victim's open mouth, propped open with a black rubber bite block similar to those used in his own office.

"Look at this." He pointed to a porcelain crown on a tooth. "See it?"

"Looks like a normal porcelain crown," Jake commented as he looked up at Mack.

"Exactly!"

"Okay, so you brought me here to look at a porcelain crown. I see those every day on my patients and might I add on live patients."

Mack laughed and turned to load an x-ray on a computer screen hanging from the wall behind the body. "Well, then what do you make of this?"

As Jake focused on the image, he saw what Mack was so excited about: a symbol on the crown.

"I found this on a routine x-ray of the mouth, hoping to get some clues to help identify this guy."

Jake had never seen such a marking on a crown before. As he focused closer on the x-ray, he realized it was more than a symbol. There were actually two letters there: A "J" superimposed over an "M". "Why would anyone take the time to do that on a crown?"

Paul Baker nodded. "We were hoping you could help us identify this guy. We found him about 5 miles outside of town, down under an old railroad bridge on the way out to Lansdun."

"I can check around with some friends at the Houston Dental School. But I've never seen this before."

Chapter 2
April 18

Dental office in Utrecht, The Netherlands

Dr. Jan Metler removed the cast crown coping from the cool water bath and began to trim the thimble shaped metal that would be the foundation for a porcelain-fused-to-metal crown. After cleaning the coping, Dr. Metler focused his attention to the metal. With meticulous care and high-powered magnification loupes, he began to cut with detail through the metal on both sides of the coping, like a master painter signing his work. He repeated this process on every crown he made. The metal etching produced a rough copy of his office logo displaying a "J" over an "M". He then applied the porcelain to the coping followed by firing in an oven to solidify the ceramic. Jan carefully took the crown and the models used to make the crown and placed them in a small plastic box where the crown would sit until the patient's appointment the next day. The name on the box was Willem Voorhis.

Jan Metler's dental practice had suffered highs and lows over the years but the last five had been very difficult financially. He had always prided himself in providing his patients with quality work, even to the extent of personally handcrafting each crown. But little by little his practice declined as the population in his area of Utrecht moved outside the city. When first contacted by his friend, Franc Liebmann, a vice president at Lansdun International, a large employer in Utrecht, about providing dental services for their employees, Jan saw a solution to his monetary concerns. Finally, this was the boost he needed, and perhaps things would be easier. After several months of a continual flow of patients from Lansdun for exams and routine dental work, Franc asked him to help with a special project. Not a problem, he remembered thinking at the time, but then he learned the details of what Franc wanted him to do. At first he thought to decline the offer, but now the money from Lansdun proved to make a dent in his financial difficulties.

Franc asked him to devise a way to transport something in the mouth of unsuspecting Lansdun trainees. When he learned that the vial to be transported was about the size of a small kernel of corn, he decided it could easily fit inside the root canal of an average molar. Intrigued by the challenge and at the same time feeling trapped in something far beyond his comfort level, Jan ignored his instinct and continued with the project.

Although he knew it was possibly wrong, unethical, and maybe even illegal, he welcomed the generous money. He justified his actions by reminding himself that Franc mentioned only four vials to transport, and then he could return to his normal practice of dentistry. In the box next to him sat crown number four.

Chapter 3
April 19

Morning shadows stretched across the town square as sunshine peaked over the trees and reflected off the dome of the old courthouse. It seemed a fairly average day as Jake parked his SUV and began the familiar walk to his office. The spring weather reminded him of the first day he opened his dental practice. How exciting and fresh it all had felt that day. Ten years had passed and he was now very much a part of Triumph.

This morning Jake pondered just how much he loved this little town. Nestled in the Piney Woods of East Texas, Triumph had the laid-back atmosphere of a small town, yet afforded its residents the amenities of Houston, 80 miles south. As with many towns in this area along the Texas - New Orleans border, it started as a center for the lumber trade and prospered until the lumber industry began to decline at the end of the 1950's. Within a decade, Triumph turned its attention to the tourist industry and, with the construction of Lake Triumph in 1965, began to prosper once again. Triumph became known as the gateway to the Forest and Lake Region of East Texas. Bed and Breakfast Inns and antique shops filled the town as it became a tourist destination. In 2000, Lansdun International, a biotechnology research company, announced it would open a research facility in Triumph. Two hundred families moved into Triumph in the fall of 2001 when the facility finally opened at the site of an abandoned paper mill. It was a tremendous boost to all aspects of the economy for the little Texas town.

Jake entered his office through the back door, glanced at the airplane ticket on his desk, stowed his briefcase in the corner and put on his white lab coat. He was anxious to start the day and get it over with so he could finish preparing for his trip to the International Dental Forum Meeting, to be held this year in Scheveningen, a seaside resort town in The Netherlands. Not only did the agenda suggest a professionally interesting meeting, but the location of the conference allowed Jake a much-needed vacation and a chance to see his grandparents. Jake knew his Oma and Opa were probably as excited about the trip as he was.

His day proved to be hectic as an already busy schedule became overwhelmed with toothache calls and patients needing to get into the office right away. It always seemed to happen, Jake thought, every time I get ready to leave town, my schedule gets loaded. Wryly, he thought there must be some sort of underground communication between his patients, triggered whenever he planned a vacation.

Sometimes he longed for the days when he used to practice in Houston. It seemed like such a long time ago, yet he had a clear memory of his years there with his wife, Annette. As newlyweds, he and Annette had bought a small house in the West University neighborhood. Together, they remodeled the post-WWII cottage, adding another bedroom to accommodate the family they dreamed of having. Yet, just four years into the dream, Jake lost Annette in an automobile accident as she visited with her parents in Arkansas. In the ten years that had passed, he often thought of what might have been. Annette would have enjoyed this trip to Europe, he thought. A smile formed on his face and distracted him from writing up patient charts.. Quickly he forced her out of his mind as he had done so many times before.

The door opened a crack after a quick knock and Franny leaned her head in, "Dr. Patterson, Mrs. Watkins is ready to get started." She stopped and peered at him. "Are you okay?"

"Yeah, Just thinking about Annette again."

Franny walked in and grabbed his hand, drew him to a standing position. "Come on, Mrs. Watkins will make you feel better. She's in a really great mood today."

As she had done many times before, Franny dragged him out of his melancholy. From the very first day he opened the doors in Triumph, she'd been his dental assistant. Her first week with him, she'd turned 21. So excited to finally be an adult, she mentioned her birthday to every patient that day. In addition to being a very adept dental assistant, Franny also set the tone in the office. Never in a bad mood, never bringing any problems from home, and never allowing others to mope, Franny filled the office with joy. Today was no different: The mood was set and all others must be joyful too.

As Jake walked with Franny toward Mrs. Watkins, his hygienist, Janna called out of her room, "Dr. Patterson, could you come and check my patient first?"

"Everything looks good here," Jake said to both Janna and her patient, snapping off his latex gloves and moving down the hall.

Once Jake had adjusted Mrs. Watkins' denture, he retired to his office to finish up details for his trip. As he studied the meeting agenda, Franny stuck her head in again. "Dr. Patterson, we have one more before lunch so don't go anywhere!"

"No problem, take an x-ray and let me know when it's on the computer," Jake replied.

In less than ten minutes Franny returned to the office, pulled up the digital x-ray on the computer and pointed. "Look at this. It's a really weird crown."

The radiograph of the tooth showed a crown with a strange symbol embedded in the middle of the restoration, exactly like the one he had seen on the man the other night in the morgue. Immediately he thought he should notify Paul about this patient, but decided he needed more information.

As he walked into the treatment room, Franny handled the introductions, "Dr Patterson, this is Peter Meijer. He's experiencing pain in his upper right 1st molar. Mr. Meijer has just arrived here from The Netherlands and has an interview over at Lansdun later this afternoon. I was just sharing with him that your mother is Dutch and that you spent a lot of time in Leiden with your grandparents."

Temporarily forgetting his tooth pain, Peter spoke, "Greetings, Doctor. Sprekken je Nederlandse?"

Jake smiled. "Ja, IkNederlandsegesprek met mijgrootouders."

"Frolijk, Doctor. Goedvoorjou." Switching to English, Peter continued, "By the way, I know Leiden. I visited there many times as a small boy. Lovely town, Leiden."

"What a small world," exclaimed Jake. "You arrive here from The Netherlands today and I'm flying over there tomorrow. But a toothache brings us together. So what seems to be the problem with your tooth?"

"Well, I've had pain ever since the root canal a month ago. The crown was put on last week before I left to come here for my interview. I just need something for the pain, please. I'll be home in two days."

During the examination Jake looked very carefully at the tooth that showed a poorly completed root canal and a crown. The crown looked normal from the outside, but the x-ray showed the unusual symbol. "Since you're just here for a few days, I can prescribe you some antibiotics and something for pain. Be sure to get that tooth checked by your dentist back home," he told the Dutch fellow.

15

Seeking more information, Jake asked, "Where did you get the crown done? As a courtesy I would like to communicate with your dentist, just to let him know you were having a problem. If you could leave his name and address I will drop him a note."

Jake figured any information he could get from the patient would be helpful to Paul. Because he had no clue what the symbol on the crown was all about, Jake decided against asking specifically about the marking. Paul will know what to do, he thought.

"Thank you doctor, I'm very grateful for your help. I'm here for an interview at Lansdun, it's the chance of a lifetime. I will leave the information with the lady at the front desk as I leave."

After saying goodbye to Mr. Meijer, Jake returned to his office and began to study the x-ray up on the computer screen. The digital x-ray allowed Jake to modify the contrast and color of the x-ray, trying his best to get a better look at the symbol. As he remembered his visit to the morgue, he wondered, "Could it be the same dentist? Do they 'sign' their work in Holland? Was the dead guy in the morgue Dutch as well?"

Jake picked up the phone and called Chief Paul Baker. The call immediately went to Paul's voicemail where Jake left a message briefly describing his encounter with his patient, as well as inquiring if the man in the morgue could also be Dutch.

Jake remembered promising Paul the other night at the morgue that he would inquire with his friend at the local dental school in Houston about the weird crown. Now he had an x-ray of another tooth just like it he could share. Jake took a moment to shoot an email and copy of the x-ray to Dr. Brennan Scott, a friend and professor at Houston Dental School.

Email: 1:30pm on Thursday April 19

To: BScott

From: JPatterson

Brennan,

I am sending you an x-ray of a patient I saw today. During the exam the crown on tooth #3 looks perfectly normal. I saw a similar x-ray with the same markings on a man in the morgue the other night as I helped the police with some dental forensics. That course you taught several years ago has resulted in more visits to the morgue than I ever wanted. My patient today is from Utrecht in the Netherlands and I am wondering if you've ever come across a marking on an x-ray like this before. Is it a European thing? Let me know what you think.

Jake

Return: 2:00pm on Thursday April 19

To: JPatterson

From: BScott

Jake,

That is some weird mark. Looks like letters or some kind of symbol. Someone would have had to go to a lot of trouble to fabricate the crown with different radiopacities. The big question is why? Let me do some research through academic channels and see what I come up with. I have a friend in Brussels at the dental school, and maybe he has seen something like this in Europe before.

Enjoy your trip! Give me a call when you get back and we can discuss your crazy crown. Maybe we can have lunch.

Brennan

Jake smiled. He enjoyed keeping in touch with Brennan. Even an email from him is a treat. He realized how much he missed seeing his old friend.

The day finished out rather routinely. That afternoon they saw eight more patients and still managed to finish on time. The staff had planned a short meeting before the end of the day to make sure everything would be handled during Dr. Patterson's vacation. They assured him that everything was under control. Franny said confidently: "We can do it Doc. Who do you think runs this office anyway?" They all laughed and exited the room.

"Dr. Patterson, are you leaving now?" called Franny on her way out the door.

"No," he said, "I just need to get a few things before I leave." The women warned him to be careful and told him to have a good time. They gathered their things and walked out of the office together. Jake followed and locked the door behind them and then went back to his office to get his briefcase. He opened the case and placed the plane tickets in the side pocket with his passport, meeting credentials, phone numbers, and an envelope with travelers' checks. He laughed at himself as he thought of how many times he had already performed the familiar routine and how many times he might repeat it before he got on the plane.

Jake left the office and retraced the short walk back to his SUV parked at the edge of the town square. He drove the eight miles out of town toward Lake Triumph to his home located right on the water. Still pondering the mark seen now on two different x-rays, he wondered what it meant to each of the men and now to him.

Chapter 4
Thursday Afternoon, April 19

Secret Lab at Lansdun Research facility in Triumph, Texas

Dr. Johann Jamison awaited his interviewee, Peter Meijer. Mr. Meijer would serve his purpose and return back to Utrecht without any knowledge that he had been used. If things progressed as scheduled he should have the necessary components needed to finish his project. While he waited, Johann recalled the last six months, back to the point when he finally had a breakthrough. Up to that time, every aspect of the project worked out except the ability to stabilize the cells indefinitely. Johann began work on the project, several years ago when he participated, on loan from Lansdun International, in a cooperative program between the Dutch and American governments designing a powerful solar battery based on the same principle as the energy generated by a cell during photosynthesis. The commercial applications of the battery, although many, were completely overlooked. The solar batteries intended use is by the military to power the necessary computer systems that a modern soldier carried at all times. Johann saw the potential for many more applications as well as a huge opportunity for personal gain. As the research continued, Johann became more and more frustrated at the limited use of the proposed application, and angered at how his ideas for other ways to use the technology were casually dismissed. He decided that if this new discovery was going to enter the open market, he had to be the one to make it happen. He knew the risks were huge, he would need to elude two governments, but the monetary payoff for Lansdun and himself would be well worth the risk. He figured all he needed was the support and help of Franc Liebmann, a vice president with the Lansdun office in Utrecht. Franc and Johann had been friends for many years and he not only knew that his friend would be interested in his proposal, but that he could be trusted

While working on the joint project at the Utrecht lab, Johann came across the breakthrough that would perfect the solar battery model. Instead of building this battery on an artificial matrix, why not build it on a wood-based matrix that would be cheap and readily available. Under proper conditions, he felt he could grow a thin sheet of cellulose several millimeters thick, then alter it to be pliable and adaptable to any surface. After the sheet of cellulose matrix was grown, the biomaterial necessary to produce the photosynthesis was interlaced upon the matrix. The matrix attached to a mesh of fine wires would direct the stored energy to any instrument or device using the power. He needed, however, an unlimited source of trees to produce enough cells to start the growth process. Then it occurred to him that Lansdun had recently opened a facility in a very wooded area of Texas, and that the laboratory had been constructed at the site of a former paper factory. The combination of many acres of forest, the proximity to the growing Biotech industry north of Houston, and the international flight in and out of Houston made a perfect spot for the new facility that would house a high security laboratory for his secret research.

Frank Liebmann embraced the idea of building a high security lab for the solar battery project, and supported using the Texas facility as the location for the lab. The project proceeded very well for the first year. Johann Jamison succeeded in building a pliable wood-based matrix from the new growth of pine trees readily accessible on the Lansdun property and the biomaterial grown did actually convert the sun's energy for the biobattery. Yet it was all very unstable and Johann became more and more frustrated in his inability to perfect a more stable battery. His project was way over budget and Franc Liebmann pressured him to get it done. Although he had completed his section of the research and development and had exited the Solarcel project, Johann was able to maintain contact with members of his former team still working with the Dutch government. With periodic conversations, he kept abreast of the progress of the government project which he used as a meter of success. Although he was working on additional research that paralleled that of the government project, his contacts were unaware of his continued involvement.

After hearing of the Solarcel project's success at developing a microscopic machine composed of live cells that was capable of making the stabilizing agent he was looking for, Johann knew what he had to do. He was so close to completion and his only obstacle was to obtain the nano-machine that Solarcel had developed. The cooperation of his ex-colleagues at Solarcel would cost a lot of money, and his only source of funds was Franc Liebmann. Johann needed to contact Franc as soon as possible, but only wanted to do it in person. He did not want to leave a trail of emails or phone calls. With the research on the wood matrix and the biomaterial on schedule, Johann had traveled back to Utrecht to meet with Franc Liebmann to discuss the final step of the project.

At first Franc Liebmann wanted nothing to do with stealing research from the government, but Johann convinced him of the need for the stabilizing agent, and reminded him that he, Johann, had developed most of the early stages of the project himself. Johann had no qualms about acquiring this last section of research by a shortcut method. The additional time it would take Johann to reach the same conclusion would end up costing Franc a similar sum of money, he reasoned with the reluctant benefactor.

So with money supplied by Liebmann from Lansdun in hand, Johann started the process of smuggling the nano-machine out of Solarcel. His contacts early on had informed him that the nano-machine was put together from four parts, all developed in separate areas at Solarcel. Getting the nano-machine was still possible but it would have to be taken out of Solarcel in four individual parts and then assembled. This twist in the obtaining the nano-machine made everything much more difficult. Not only would they have to smuggle something out of Solarcel, but they would have to do it four times. In addition to that, the smuggled parts of the nano-machine needed to be replicated and kept alive until the machine was complete and ready to produce the stabilizer. The secret lab at the Texas facility was perfect for growing and keeping the parts of the nano-machine, but Johann's big questions centered around how to get the samples to Texas and how to get them there alive.

Johann's contacts at Solarcel informed him that the cells were most stable at human body temperature and would remain alive for 48 to 72 hours. The cells were taken out of Solarcel in small glass vials containing a liquid that had a high concentration of cells complete with the recipe to keep them healthy in the lab and how to stimulate the cells to grow. Johann determined that a good way to smuggle the cell concentrate into the United States and to the facility at Lansdun in Triumph was inside the human mouth. This method would provide a warm and stable environment. Yet, this method required the cooperation and involvement of more individuals, substantially increasing the risk of detection or failure.

Liebmann insisted that every aspect of the movement of the cell concentrate needed to appear legitimate to all outside eyes. Johann quickly came up with a scheme to allow unsuspecting individuals to carry the nano-machine parts through customs and into the United States. As the idea developed further, Johann and Franc decided they would recruit men to smuggle the material to Texas by offering them a chance for a job. Before they sent them to the interview in Texas the men would be required as "company policy" to get a medical and dental exam. The first part of the nano-machine would be available in 30 days and little time could be wasted. Johann returned to Texas to set up the changes necessary in the lab to support the smuggled microscopic components. His contacts would get the cell concentrate out of the Solarcel project but it was up to Franc Liebmann to figure out how to smuggle the glass vials from Utrecht to Texas.

Franc thought through the scheme that he and Johann had planned. His concerns were lifted as he thought of the dentist that recently began doing exams and treatment for Lansdun, Dr. Jan Metler. Perhaps he could convince his friend Jan to help him figure out a way to transport (he hated to think of himself as a smuggler) the glass vials undetected.

Chapter 5
Hollenvat Estate Outside of Amsterdam

Growing up in a wealthy Dutch family certainly had its benefits, but now that Willem Van Hollenvat was approaching his twenty-first birthday, he was anxious for a new life. He wanted to find out what it might be like to live an ordinary life. Willem thought back to the many difficult conversations he had with his father where he tried to convince his father that he needed to be out on his own, not dependent on the family money. But his father would not hear it, his whole life was planned for him. He was to go to the Leiden University, major in Biochemistry and Business, then after graduation go to work in the family business where he would be groomed to take over someday. Willem's father, Rijkaard, was CEO of Lansdun International, a biotechnology firm headquartered in Amsterdam near Schiphol airport. Willem had been surrounded by the company his whole life and wasn't sure he felt led to ever run his father's company. The path of his future was his own decision. He desired to experience what it would be like to work for something and actually earn money. During his whole life, everything had been given to him. Now it was time to break away from the life that had been so carefully planned for him, and make some choices for himself.

He had been planning his escape for a long time and before he knew it, his twenty first birthday arrived. After the family party he planned to slip away and begin his adventure. No longer the son of Rijkaard Van Hollenvat, this night he would begin a journey as Willem Voorhis, a common man. The planning had been meticulous and detailed, capped off with a new passport as Willem Voorhis.

Two weeks ago, Willem had interviewed for the job at Lansdun International's location in Utrecht. Here he hoped no one would recognize him or even suspect he was the owner's son. Surprised when he was hired on the spot and even more surprised when he got scheduled to travel to the United States to interview for a position in the Triumph, Texas, research facility. He laughed when he thought how over qualified he was for the lab tech post. With three years of college Biochemistry behind him, this job would be easier than a freshman level chemistry or biology class. In the past two weeks he had received training as an entry-level lab technician in order to prepare for the interview in Texas. At the same time, he took the mandatory medical and dental exams he needed to qualify for the trip. The training proved simple and sometimes monotonous, yet for the first time in his life he felt genuinely excited.

The family birthday party consisted of the usual guests and fanfare, but although he had a wonderful time, Willem was ready for the next leg of his adventure. Each time the guest wished "Gelukkige Verjaardag" throughout the evening he heard it as "bon voyage." By the time the last guest left the family estate around 11:30pm, Willem had already told his parents of his plans to go out with friends after the party to continue the celebration. They knew he was due to be back in school at Leiden University for the remainder of the spring session, so he added that he would spend the night with his friends in town and then travel back in the morning. With the goodbyes over, now all he had to do was disappear into his new life.

For the next few weeks, he had to be very careful. The last thing he needed was for someone to get word to his parents of his job at Lansdun. The plan seemed to be progressing very well, he would stay in contact with his parents just like he always did while away at school, never giving a hint about his employment at the facility in Utrecht several hours away from school. Only his roommate back at school knew of his plan and he had agreed to keep Willem's secret. Once he got the job in the United States, Willem would contact his parents and tell them the story.

Chapter 6
Friday Morning

Jake woke up early the next morning, as excited as a child ready to begin his trip. He was ticketed to fly on Continental Airlines Flight #46 from Houston Intercontinental Airport to Schiphol Airport leaving at 7:40pm Houston time and arriving in Amsterdam at 11:50am the next day Netherlands time. He began packing several days before but now he added the last few things and closed the suitcase. It was 10am and if he left soon he would have more time to spend with his sister Lauren before she dropped him off at the airport. He originally had intended on parking at the airport, but his sister insisted he come by, visit for a while, and then she would take him to the airport. After one last look around the house, Jake locked the doors, gathered his bags and briefcase and loaded them in the back of the SUV. He climbed into the car, drove around the circular driveway, and out to the farm-to-market road to begin the ninety minute drive to Houston. After a series of familiar back roads, Jake accelerated onto Highway 59 as he headed towards Houston. He turned off of the highway into a neighborhood nestled along the San Jacinto River where his sister lived with her family. He drove through the tree-lined streets and had to admit that it really was convenient that his sister and her husband Steve lived so close to the airport.

As he pulled into the driveway, he saw his twin blond-headed nieces playing in the front yard. Ashley and Marley, age five, were dressed in matching denim overalls with different pastel colored t-shirts. As soon as they recognized his car, they bolted toward the driveway squealing, "Yippee! Yea! Uncle Jake's here!" As quickly as he stopped, the girls had his door open and were climbing into his lap.

"Uncle Jake, what did you bring us?" blurted Ashley.

"Nothing yet girls, I haven't taken my trip yet, but I promise I will bring you something." Jake explained in a patient tone.

Just then the twin's mother came out the front door to greet him. "Girls, Girls, give Uncle Jake a chance to get out of the car." She walked up to Jake as he emerged, gave him a hug and a peck on the cheek. "How you doing, Hon?"

Jake responded with a "Great! Ready to Go!"

"Oh, I'm so jealous, Jake. Do you know how long it's been since I've visited Oma and Opa? I'd love to take the girls over there. Right, girls?"

"We want to go to Holland!" The girls began to chant, "We wanna go to Holland, we wanna go to Holland," all the way into the house.

"Where's Steve? Why would anyone work on this nice Friday afternoon?"

"Unfortunately, he is. Some people still have to work on Fridays, you know," she teased. "He was hoping to be here but he had a huge court case all week. The girls and I have hardly seen him at all. He asked me to wish you 'Bon Voyage'. "

Lauren and Steve Page had been married for ten years. They met not long after Steve was hired as an attorney for Texan Oil. In fact, their large church wedding in Houston had been the last time the family had seen Annette. The day after the wedding she left for Arkansas to visit her parents.

The girls led Jake into the family room where he took a seat on the couch. As they climbed into his lap, Jake handed his sister a copy of his itinerary and asked if she had any messages for Oma and Opa. Lauren just sighed, "I sure wish I could go see them again. They're not getting any younger. Maybe next year! I haven't seen them since Mom and Dad's funeral."

His parents insisted he move into their lake house after Annette's death. The comfortable vacation home on the lake was the perfect place for Jake to be alone in his loss. When the local dentist decided to retire a short time after Jake's arrival, he considered it a blessing to have an opportunity to start over in the town where he had so many good memories. Jake bought the practice and began his life in Triumph. Since Jake's parents, John and Cora Patterson, had relocated 10 years earlier to Central America in Tegucigalpa, Honduras, they were in no hurry to evict their son from the family cabin. Starting with Texan Oil right out of college, Jake's dad had risen quickly in the company. He transferred in and out of Texas over his career, including the two year assignment in the Netherlands where he met Cora, fell in love, and married. Although their family bounced all over the United States, the Pattersons considered Houston their hometown. Even when they lived in another state or city, they could always return to the quiet town of Triumph for a much needed vacation at the house overlooking the lake.

The promotion and move to Honduras made John Patterson President of Texan Oil's Central American ventures. The Tegucigalpa location, a 4 hour flight from Houston, was close to where they enjoyed vacationing in the Caribbean when they could not get back to Triumph. Although Jake and Lauren missed their parents, their move did provide the family with new opportunities. Jake remembered the day his parents bought the home in a little place he had never heard of: Ambergris Caye, near San Pedro Town in Belize. "Come to Belize," they phoned him in Triumph. "We bought another retreat." After a 2 1/2 hour plane ride from Houston to Belize International Airport on TACA and a 20 minute flight in a Tropic Air puddle jumper, he landed on a dusty little airstrip that looked more like a long driveway than an actual runway. He was met at the plane by his parents and whisked away to a boat waiting at the dock about 50 yards from the "airport." After a twenty minute boat ride, they arrived at the house his parents bought as a "retreat." Some retreat, he thought as he got off the boat at the side of the long, wooden pier and had his first glimpse of the five bedroom, tile roofed house just 30 yards from the water. "So this is what paradise looks like," he remarked to his parents.

John and Cora Patterson died just three months later when the corporate plane they were flying in crashed, leaving no survivors. The phone call came to Jake back in Triumph on a cool September night as he was coming in from an afternoon of fishing with a new friend, Paul Baker, the Triumph police chief. Shortly after coming to Triumph, he and Paul had met at a Chamber of Commerce function, where, after realizing they both had grown up in Houston, began to build a close friendship. Paul Baker was in his early 40s and had recently retired from 20 years on the Houston Police Force. He ended his career there as a detective and department liaison to the FBI. Upon retirement he was not ready to give up on police work, his love and passion, so when the job opened up in Triumph he gladly took it. Jake and Paul had just set down their fishing tackle when the phone rang.

"Jake," Lauren asked with a crack in her voice. "It's mom and dad. There's been an accident." As quickly as he heard the words, memories of the call about Annette filled his heart. The tone sounded familiar and he braced himself for the news.

"Mom and Dad's plane went down. They were traveling to Panama. There were no survivors." Tearfully she continued, "Jake, Mom and Dad are gone."

The next few weeks proved very difficult and Jake was glad Paul was there to help him with all the details of getting their bodies back in the country. Paul's connections were amazing, and Jake saw that people seemed to really want to do whatever Paul asked.

After a beautiful funeral, Jake, Lauren, and her husband traveled to Belize to spread their parent's ashes on the beach of the retreat they had so enjoyed. After they returned home they worked to settle the estate and discovered that their Mom and Dad had built a very healthy sum for Jake and Lauren to inherit. With the estate and the money from the company's insurance, Jake, Lauren and her family would always be taken care of. There was even a provision in the will that would provide and take care of the homes at San Pedro and on Lake Triumph. Jake and Lauren were debt free. They had always led a privileged life, but now any worries they might come to have for their financial future were taken care of. Texan Oil had been good to his father.

After getting caught up on the family over a quick lunch Jake felt the need to start heading toward the airport. His sister laughed and told him not to be so neurotic about getting there early, but she knew better than to try to stall him. She helped the girls buckle up in Jake's SUV and they began the short trip.

In only twenty minutes, Jake pulled in to the drop off lane at the International Terminal of the Houston Intercontinental Airport, got out of the driver side and met Lauren at the back of the vehicle. He opened the hatch and blew kisses to Ashley and Marley. One last hug for Lauren and he gathered up his bags and headed into the terminal. He turned and waved goodbye as they drove off. Since he had arrived early, there were no lines or delays and he wished his sister could see how easily he got checked in and through security, due of course, to his meticulous planning. He headed up the escalator to his gate and decided to stop at the magazine rack to shop and stock up on gum, mints and anything else to occupy himself during the long trip. He picked out a paperback thriller, piled his selections on the small checkout counter and presented his credit card, pleased that the trip had officially begun. As he turned from the counter he bumped into a woman.

Before he could get out an "excuse me Ma'am," he heard, "Dr. Patterson, what are you doing here?"

31

Jake smiled as he recognized Kate Williams. "Well I – I'm getting ready to take a trip."

Kate reddened, "I guess that was a stupid question, of course you're going on a trip." Katherine Williams was a resident of Triumph, and one of Jake's patients. He remembered her first appointment at his office. That day he felt instant chemistry and only the second time in his life that he felt an immediate attraction for a woman. The first time was with his wife, Annette, in Spanish 101 at Baylor University during his freshman year. Over the past two years, he seemed to run into Kate almost everywhere he turned. At church, Chamber of Commerce functions, the Rotary Club, and even in the grocery store; however, with all the contact and the attraction that he knew they both felt, Jake still couldn't allow himself to get closer. Although he hung on to the notion that he didn't need to get involved with one of his patients, he had to admit it had more to do with being scared. He knew a relationship with Kate could be serious and that alarmed him. He feared an involvement with Kate would replace his memories of Annette and even after ten years, he could not bear to let her memory just fade away.

As usual, Jake made small talk and ended the encounter with a "Have a great trip, Kate. I'll see you back in Triumph." He smiled again, turned and left the store. This time, however, he felt immediate frustration and he walked away irritated that he hadn't at least asked her to sit with him for coffee or a drink. He walked to the gate and took a seat, tried to concentrate on his new book, and did not look up until it was announced that it was time to board his flight.

Kate paid for her magazine and proceeded to her gate. She too was disappointed that their conversation had ended so abruptly and yet hoped there would be another time to get to know this interesting man. She had only been in Triumph for about two years and Dr. Jake Patterson was the most intriguing man she had met in a long time. Looking back at the events that led her to Triumph, she never dreamed her high profile corporate job would ever take her to a small community in Texas. At the time, it was just what she needed. Kate had married right after graduate school to a man who just happened to be in the right place at the right time, she had come to conclude. There was nothing really wrong with her relationship with Tony, other than the fact that they had no relationship. Not long after what she came to see as an obligatory wedding following her graduation from college, both she and Tony found that their respective careers left them with little time to spend together. So after their 3-year marriage dissolved, she was alone and wholly focused on her work. At this time she was guarded to let any annoyance, even men, distract her, so she was a bit surprised that she had felt an attraction to Dr. Patterson.

The focus had paid off professionally, however, and soon Kate found herself in a role as an Assistant Director of Operations for Lansdun International's facility located in New Brunswick, New Jersey. After several years in New Jersey she was transferred to the new Texas plant and promoted to Director of Operations. At first she was upset that the move would sidetrack her career, but on the plus side, the move got her further away from her ex-husband's family who had never accepted the fact that Kate was no longer interested in their attentions. Just a few weeks after her move to Triumph, Kate felt right at home. The small, quiet community north of Houston was just what she needed. When she craved the city life, Houston was close by and she still had the opportunity to travel with her new position so she never had the feeling that she was stuck in a small town. Rather, it became a quiet sanctuary away from the hustle and bustle of the corporate world. It wasn't until she first met Dr. Patterson that she even considered that something was still missing from her life. Although she didn't really know what to expect from men in Texas, Jakob Patterson struck her as educated, refined, and even sophisticated, but with less "attitude" than the men she had known back in Boston. Yet despite how many times she ran into him, he seemed overly shy or distant. Whereas she might have been discouraged, Kate simply felt more determined to get to know him.

Chapter 7
Kate's Transfer to Triumph

Kate's move to Triumph turned out to be the right step in her career. As Director of Operations, she was responsible for plant operations. Her years of experience with Lansdun had earned her the trust of her regional manager, so Kate ran the Texas branch with almost total autonomy. All the reports that she sent to her boss in New Jersey showed that she was managing the Texas location like a seasoned professional. Although she knew little of the research end of the company, she usually was able to grasp the basics of the projects they were working on. Her responsibilities included virtually every aspect of the daily operation of the facility. She worked very hard to stay abreast of each new project and was welcomed by every department as she sought answers to any questions she might have.

The previous year, a new research wing at the plant had opened up. Although Kate was in charge of all operations for the facility, this area of the plant was out of her jurisdiction. It had a separate entrance to the rear of the facility, a separate phone system, a separate computer line, and she had no idea who actually worked there. The employees of the wing did share the company cafeteria but kept to themselves behind the semi-opaque screen that had been set up in one corner of the room. After questioning her boss as to why she had no authority over the lab, she found out it was a restricted, high-security project that had its own Operations Manager. She did not have security clearance, nor would she ever need to enter that wing of the facility. "They won't bother you," she was told. Though irritated, she was forced to accept the independence of the research wing. Regularly, she was aware that her supplies were acquisitioned by the wing, causing a shortage in her inventory. And that did bother her.

One day at lunch, Kate glanced across the room toward the smoked glass of the private dining area, only to recognize a familiar face. Buck McFadden recognized Kat and smiled, but quickly turned away, as he ducked behind the glass screen. "How strange," Kate thought. "We were such good friends in New Brunswick. Why didn't Buck tell me he was here?" Briefly troubled by this apparent snub by an old friend, she returned to her office to finish her work and prepared to leave earlier than usual.

Shortly, Kate left work to drive the 10 miles to her little cottage nestled near a small cove on the eastern edge of Lake Triumph. Most of the rooms looked out over the lake, but at the back of the house was her favorite spot: a screened in porch that provided safety from the Texas mosquitoes and yellow jackets, yet gave her the feel of the outdoors that she loved so much. As she turned into her driveway, she couldn't wait to change into a t-shirt and jeans, pour a glass of wine, and head out to the porch. The anticipation of this daily ritual totally erased any irritation about her encounter with Buck.

Kate parked in the garage, gathered her purse and briefcase, and proceeded back up the driveway to collect her mail from the box on the street. As she headed for the front door she noticed a small blue envelope stuck in the screen door. When she opened the door the envelope fell to the floor and she saw it was simply addressed to "Kate." Immediately, she recognized Buck's handwriting. Kate walked in, headed straight toward the fireplace-accented den, kicked off her shoes, dropped her things on the leather sofa and sat down to read the note.

Kate,

Email tonight. I will be waiting. Use your personal email not Lansdun. Urgent that you email tonight to <u>BuckyM.</u>. Destroy this note immediately.

Buck

Surprised and somewhat frightened by his tone in the note, Kate got up and locked the front door, then headed down the short hallway to the small alcove office nestled next to her bedroom. After turning on the computer, Kate sat down to write an email to Buck.

BuckyM

Buck,

What's up? Why the cloak and dagger secrecy? Is this a game?

Kate

Buck quickly replied as if he had been waiting for Kate to get home from work. Kate opened and began to read an email that would change her quiet little world forever.

KateW

Kate,

It was sure great to see you at the cafeteria today. I knew you were here and have wanted to contact you since I got here four weeks ago. I've been under careful watch since I have arrived and have not even been able to call you. All outside calls to and from our department are screened and we are told not to make contact with anyone in the building. I wanted to talk to you when I saw you today, but it's not safe. I took a big risk leaving the note. Even now I am writing this from a public computer at the Triumph library.

Something is just not right. We are working with material that has been smuggled into the facility and I suspect that the work I'm involved in is illegal. The stuff is coming from a lab in Utrecht, maybe from within Lansdun. Not sure how it is getting here, but it arrives in very small quantities. I thought maybe you'd know what to do. Check your email often. Erase this email when you are done.

Buck

Respecting Buck's computer expertise and advice, Kate closed the email address on her computer and quickly took steps to erase all trace of the email or the IP address that might show up on her computer's internet history. She made a mental note not to check her email from her laptop at work. Her department managed all the Information Systems at her facility in Triumph and although she was not a "computer geek," she still knew enough about computers to remove any easy trace that she had opened Buck's email and to know that there could be many eyes watching on the Lansdun network.

Alarmed and concerned, Kate began to look out for things that seemed out of the ordinary. Although she checked her email several times a day for another communication from Buck, it was several weeks before he contacted her again. She might have dismissed his first email as a joke or just a way to get her attention, but while she waited to hear from him, she began to notice items missing from the inventory, unauthorized shipments being unloaded, and then mysteriously disappearing.

To: KateW

From: BuckyM

Subject: Urgent!!!!!!!!

Kate,

Need to meet! Tonight! Starlight Café on the town square. 9pm.

Buck

Later that evening Kate walked into the Starlight Café, still wondering what Buck was getting her involved in. As she entered in the front door of the café, the warm cozy atmosphere surprised her, and she wondered why she had never been there before. The interior of the café was a flashback to the fifties with the broad L shaped lunch counter bordered by six stools placed at its edge. Across from the counter was a row of four booths and in the back was a section that had about 10 tables, each with four chrome-legged chairs. The walls displayed photos of the history of the lumber industry that once dominated the town. She could picture the café filled each morning and the buzz of conversation that kept all of the townsfolk up to date on Triumph's current events. Buck stood in the back corner waving at her. He sat back down, spilling his cup of coffee, and proceeded to wipe up the mess, oblivious of the courtesies one would give a woman joining him at the table. Buck showed every bit of his 57 years, with a stringy "comb-over" and 40 extra pounds. He wore corduroys, a white open collar shirt and a light brown cardigan, buttoned up. His bifocals rested halfway down his nose. He was truly a caricature of a computer geek.

As Kate sat down, he looked up with a sad smile and said, "Kate, I really hated to get you involved but I had nowhere else to turn. Something is really wrong over there and I just can't figure it out. I think they know I'm suspicious, but I don't think they know I've emailed you."

"I don't know what I can do for you, Buck," Kate replied.

He looked down at the table. "I just need someone to talk to. Before I do, I have to tell you that there's a possibility that this information may put you in danger."

"What are you talking about? What kind of danger?"

"I'm not even sure about that. But I really need to talk to you."

Sitting across the table from a man she knew was in the habit of overreacting to every change in his life, Kate decided to let him talk. After all, he had spent the entire month of December, 1999, backing up his computer files in anticipation of the expected Y2K disasters. Buck's idea of danger was very different from that of most people.

"Go ahead," she encouraged him.

Buck took a deep breath and reached for a paper napkin from the dispenser on the table. Wiping perspiration from his forehead, he told her about the secret project in his department - a solar battery involving nanobots, living cells working together as microscopic machines. He continued to explain that his role in the lab was technical support for the large computer system running the research. To Kate, it seemed that Buck had free reign of the facility except for where the most secret part of the project was conducted in a locked and guarded laboratory. On one occasion, he got to enter the separate lab when he had to service one of the computers there. The security cameras and the guards carefully watched him the entire time he worked on the computer.

"Kate, as best as I can figure it out from what I've seen and the computer programs I monitor, the research has some military significance. It appears things are coming to a climax. The puzzling part about the project is the test matter appears from nowhere. No requisition, no order form, no label, nothing but just tiny glass containers that are tightly sealed and only about 5mm square.

"Kate, these glass containers are filled with small microscopic nanobots that are 'alive'. I've never seen anything like it before in any other lab, but apparently these nanobots can be controlled and told what to do. Every precaution is taken not to touch them or they'll become contaminated," Buck explained.

"I can't possibly figure out where or how they're appearing because from what I have seen, they need to be kept in a moist environment about 98.6 degrees. Even the slightest variance from that temperature causes them to die or cease to work. They never arrive in our normal biomedical shipments.

"Here's the weird part, I think they're smuggled into the facility. During the last couple of months, Dutch nationals, from our Utrecht office, show up here for an interview or something. During the tour of the facility, each one is taken into closed section of the laboratory for about an hour, and then leaves the lab, somewhat disoriented, for what I can only guess is the return trip to Utrecht. Every time, I overhear Dr. Johann Jamison, the project manager, saying he will contact them soon. The strange thing is, with all of the applicants interviewed, you'd think they would hire one of them."

Kate had to admit that it was a disturbing set of circumstances. With her curious observations as of late, Kate, while alarmed, did not perceive the level of danger that seemed to make him afraid. She told Buck ever since his first email she had been watching very carefully for a pattern of irregularity that could be traced to the special research section.

"And the only thing I notice out of place is in inventory and shipping, when some items appear and disappear," she said. "It's nothing that I could really pinpoint as too weird, but it drives me crazy. You know how I am about keeping up with details. I'm supposed to know where everything is, where it came from and where it's going. That's my job."

"Well I hope I haven't scared you too much with all this, how did you put it? Oh yeah, 'cloak and dagger' secrecy. Really, Kate, I thought you'd take this more seriously. Just keep your eyes open and let me know what you find out. Be sure to use your private email. You really need to be careful; this is dangerous Kate. It may be 'cloak and dagger' for real. I may regret getting you involved in this - I don't want you to get hurt. You're special to me, Kate."

With that last comment Buck got up and darted out of the cafe without looking back, leaving Kate to pay for his coffee and ponder his last statement.

This morning before she left for the airport, Kate received another email from Buck.

To: KateW

From: BuckyM

Subject: Urgent!!!!!!!!

Kate,

I have been asked to go to Utrecht. I will email you when I get back.

Buck

Chapter 8
Houston Intercontinental Airport – International Terminal

Kate walked down the terminal to board her flight and as she approached the gate to her flight, she saw him. Jake was seated near the airline desk and had obviously fallen asleep while reading his book. As she walked up to him, she noticed the airplane ticket in his pocket, a first class ticket for the same flight she was on. She looked up to double check the sign at the gate. "Flight 46 to Amsterdam, leaving at 7:40pm," she read. "I'm in the right place." She stole another look at the sleeping Jake. Suddenly she had an idea and hurried to the airline counter at the gate. "I hope you can help me." She smiled at the attendant, then said, "My colleague and I had hoped to get seats together but were told to contact the desk at the gate. We're both traveling first class. Are there any seats together?"

"What is your friend's name?" asked the lady behind the counter.

"Jake Patterson"

"Ok, here he is! He is in row 4a, right by the window and there is a seat next to him. Will that work for you?"

"That would be perfect." Kate tried to hide her delight.

"Alright then, you are moved to 4B. Is there anything else I can do for you?"

"No Ma'am, everything's just fine."

The woman responded with a knowing smile, pleased that she had just helped a passenger prepare for their voyage.

Jake was awakened from his unexpected nap by the PA system announcing his flight. Falling asleep had not been in his plan at all. He gathered his things and hurried to the men's room, never noticing Kate sitting in the corner of the waiting area, trying very hard to remain invisible. Kate saw this as her opportunity to surprise him and was first in line for the first class cabin seating. She made it on board and was seated in 4B long before Jake came rushing back to the gate.

As he approached his seat Jake could see that 4B was already occupied and he wondered who he would be stuck sitting next to for ten hours. When he reached his seat, his heart skipped a beat when he saw Kate. This really will be a first class flight was his only thought as he froze speechless in the aisle. Kate smiled and got up to let him in to his seat.

After an awkward moment, Jake broke the silence. "Well, this is certainly a coincidence. I had no idea you were going to The Netherlands. What are you doing in Europe? How long will you be there?"

"Whoa, Whoa, too many questions too fast, we have ten hours to talk," Kate responded with a laugh.

"Well, I guess you are right about that. We do have a lot of time to get acquainted."

As the plane taxied to the runway, they began to share their destinations, purposes for their trips, and how long they would be away. "What are the chances we'd be sitting together," remarked Jake. "This is wild!"

Kate shrugged. "Makes you believe that some things are just meant to be."

When Jake had let Kate walk away from him at the news stand, he thought he had missed a golden opportunity. Now he found himself in her company for ten whole hours. What else is meant to be? Jake mused.

"Now, Kate, I remember from your visit to my office that you're originally from Beacon Hill in Boston, right."

"Wow! I'm touched you remember that about me considering the number of patients you must see every day. Yes, I grew up in Bean Town, on Beacon Hill; a real city girl."

"Tell me about the life of Kate Williams."

"Oh, there's not much more. That was then, this is now." She laughed. "What could you possible want to know?"

"How about, everything in between?"

"Well, I suppose we do have a lot of time to fill. Where shall I start?"

"Family?"

"My dad was a financial analyst - medical acquisitions and mergers. My mom balanced stay at home mom and real estate. I have two sisters and I'm in the middle. We had a pretty normal life. As a little girl, my passions were choir, cheerleading, and soccer. I graduated salutatorian of my high school class and then went to Boston University for my B.A. in Business, then I enrolled at Harvard and left a couple of years later with an MBA in Finance and Human Resources. I was offered my current job right out of graduate school and the rest is history. That's my story and I'm sticking to it. What's yours?"

Jake purposely began his story in the present, explaining the details of his trip to attend a meeting of the International Dental Forum meeting near The Hague, in the seaside town of Scheveningen. He also told her about his Oma and Opa, in the town of Leiden, only 20 minutes by train from The Hague. He was spending the first few nights at the convention hotel, the Kurhaus Hotel in Scheveningen, then he was going to spend the remainder of the trip in Leiden with family.

"Family in Europe!" Kate exclaimed. "How romantic. Your mom's parents, I assume."

"That's right. My father's family is all in Texas. Dad met Mother when he went to Holland on a special assignment for his company, Texan Oil, to work with the Royal Dutch Oil company. One day, he took a tourist trip to The Keukenhof, where Mother was working that spring. Their story had always been 'love at first sight'. Or at least that's what they told me and Lauren. My sister and I asked our grandparents to take us out to the Keukenhof every time we visited them. Each time we acted out Mom and Dad's first meeting, we got sillier and sillier."

"The Keukenhof! I've heard so much about it. I would love to go there."

"I hope you'll have time to enjoy yourself in Holland. Do you have a full schedule?" Kate explained that she was going to Utrecht for a biannual meeting at Lansdun International headquarters. "This is my third trip to The Netherlands, but I've never had a chance to see any of the country."

"That's a shame to travel all that distance and not be able to enjoy it. I would love to show you around if you can spare a few days. We could meet in Leiden and visit with my grandparents. You would enjoy meeting them. And The Keukenhof is only minutes away from Leiden. We could easily make a trip there."

Kate, clearly excited, vowed to work a side trip into her schedule, no matter what. They immediately exchanged cell numbers, addresses, and email addresses. Kate and Jake talked without stopping for the next five hours, only allowing interruptions from the flight attendant who was busy providing them with meals, drinks, and snacks - all the amenities of first class service.

As the lights of the cabin dimmed, Jake and Kate were beginning to see that this time together on the flight was building into something they both wanted to last for a long time. The busyness of the day getting to the airport began to settle in on their bodies and they both drifted off to sleep as the big jetliner flew across the ocean. Kate kicked off her shoes and curled up on the reclining seat with Jake next to her.

A few hours later, Jake woke up to find Kate still asleep. He was close enough to smell her perfume and her hair, giving him a feeling of comfort that he had not experienced in a very long time. Unable to go back to sleep, Jake spent the next hour studying every aspect of her perfect complexion. The sound of her gentle breathing gave him a peace he knew was missing from his life.

Too soon for Jake, Kate woke from her slumber as the plane rumbled from slight turbulence. Her eyes opened to find Jake staring at her. "I'm glad we're here to together," he whispered.

"Me too," replied Kate.

At that moment, Jake leaned over, put two fingers under her chin, lifting it up to kiss Kate gently on the lips. Kate responded as Jake had hoped she would, and suddenly his self-imposed dating policy evaporated somewhere over the Atlantic Ocean. In the semi-darkness, the kiss turned passionate, with both Jake and Kate wishing that they weren't stuck on a plane, first class or not.

"Meant to be?" Jake asked.

"That's how I see it." Kate sighed and put her head on his shoulder.

To an observer, the remainder of the flight appeared rather uneventful as the couple watched the in-flight movie. But to Kate and Jake, their time together marked the beginning of something very special.

Before long, the voice of the flight attendant announced instructions for landing at Schiphol airport. As the passengers prepared for landing, the flight attendants began their final pass through the cabin. The plane began to decelerate and lose altitude, and Jake could see out the window the miniature shapes of the country he loved to visit. The day looked to be typical Netherlands weather, with an overcast sky and a breeze blowing in off the frigid North Sea coast, making Jake wish the meeting had been scheduled in August, the country's only warm month. Although decidedly cool, Jake had always loved the time of year when the flowers began to bloom and the colors of the country came to life. As he thought of this trip and the last ten hours on the plane, he smiled and gently touched Kate's arm. She woke up with a smile on her face and leaned in for one more kiss, a quick kiss, but one full of meaning. They both knew it signaled the beginning of their new relationship.

"This changes the focus of my trip somewhat." Kate smiled at Jake. "I'll be counting the days until I can see you again.

"Another coincidence," Jake exclaimed. "I was going to say just the same thing!"

The landing was long and smooth with hardly a squeak of tires as the plane touched ground.

As they departed the plane, Jake practiced the gentlemanly skills he had not used for a very long time. He retrieved Kate's carryon luggage and remembered the "ladies first" custom in the aisle. As they reached the terminal from the gangway, Jake grabbed Kate's hand, still reluctant to let the trip come to an end.

The plane had pulled into terminal D which meant a long walk to the baggage claim area. As they rounded the first bend hand in hand, ahead of them lay long moving sidewalks on each side of the wide corridor. The automated reminder continually repeated in Dutch-accented English, "Watch your step!" To both Jake and Kate, it sounded more like, "Wash yotep, wash yotep, washyotep!" The familiar greeting made Jake feel at home.

Soon they arrived at the baggage claim where they picked up their bags and made their way to Customs and Immigration. Jake led the way and got to the customs official first. Although English was spoken throughout the country, Jake, fluent in Dutch, seemed to leave English behind and transform himself into a Dutch National. With his short blond hair, 6'2" height, and bright blue eyes, Jake easily passed as a hometown boy from Leiden. Kate was amazed by Jake's transformation as he conversed in Dutch.

After a leisurely lunch at one of the restaurants at the airport, Jake announced it was time to purchase their train tickets.

"I'm not ready to go yet, Jake. I can't believe that I'm already dreading being apart from you."

"I feel the same way, but we'll be together in a few days. Won't it be great to have our meetings out of the way? Come on, the ticket booth is just right around that corner."

She sighed. "I guess the sooner we get going the sooner we can be together again."

Jake led Kate around the corner and walked up to the counter.

"You know, you are quite handy to have around in this country. I'm looking forward to taking advantage of all your talents." She stated as she winked at Jake.

With a grin, Jake replied, "Oh, really?"

"What I meant, of course, was I want you to buy my ticket. You speak perfect Dutch. One 1st Class ticket to Utrecht, please," she said as they stood at the ticket counter.

"You've got to be kidding." Jake laughed. "1st Class, Why 1st class? I always travel 2nd Class. You get to mingle and see the people and learn a little more about the country. Trust me - it'll be much better."

Jake turned toward the cashier and requested the two different tickets. Hers to Utrecht and his to The Hague. "Iktehebbengelieveéénkaartjeaan Den Haag en nodigaanbeide Utrecht, tweedeklasse." He paid with Euros and gave Kate her change. With tickets in hand Jake went over the details of Kate's journey.

"You'll change trains in Amsterdam. It should be easy to find the train to Utrecht. There should be one leaving every 30 minutes. Look for the express – the snell train, not the one that stops at each town."

"I think I can figure it out."

Jake looked at his watch and said," I think we better go down to the platform now."

Once there, he set down her luggage, then turned to Kate and pulled her toward him for a farewell embrace. He kissed her gently and whispered in her ear, "This day has been amazing. I'll see you in a few days. In the meantime, take care. Please call me when you get to your hotel in Utrecht."

Kate was touched by his concern for her safety. She could not remember the last time anyone cared about her in such a way. She could hardly wait to get to her hotel and call him.

The sound of rumbling filled the platform as the yellow train arrived at the station. It came to a stop and they moved directly in front of a #2, or second class train. As the doors opened, Kate kissed Jake again and stepped into the train. Jake followed to place her luggage inside the car. "See you soon!' he said as he quickly exited, waving as the doors closed and the train started down the track.

Kate took a seat by the window for the 45 minute ride to Utrecht. Gazing at the beautiful Dutch countryside, she reflected on the surprising turn her life had taken in the past twenty four hours. She had long been curious about the handsome, quiet, young dentist, but never imagined she would get to know him so quickly or so well.

Jake boarded his train to The Hague and settled in for the 40 minute commute on the express train. He arrived at The Hague Central Station and then with a quick hail of a cab he was on his way to the Kurhaus Hotel in Scheveningen, home this week to the International Dental Forum. The meetings would start tomorrow and Jake looked forward to the new insights he might gain from the speakers.

Soon after he checked into his room at the Kurhaus, he received a call from Kate on his cell phone. While he had looked forward to hearing her voice again, he had a momentary flash of panic. Would it be an awkward conversation with a woman he had kissed on a plane? After all, a transatlantic trip, the jetlag and time changes are far different from the events of real life. Had his loneliness finally gotten the better of him, and Kate just happened to be there? He needn't have worried, however. The phone call picked up their day where it had left off at the train station. What could have been a very uncomfortable situation was instead just the opposite, an intimate conversation that neither wanted to end.

The next morning, Jake checked into the dental meeting and noted the wide variety of interesting topics. For Jake, the highlight of any dental meeting was always the exhibit hall where he could see the newest equipment and gadgets. But this time, Jake could think of nothing but Kate. It was only 10:00 am and already the Dental Forum held no excitement for him . Even a walk through exhibits turned out to be no fun. All he could think about was their last phone call.

On Sunday and Monday, both Jake and Kate made an attempt to participate in the meetings they had traveled so far to attend. Somehow for Jake, crown and bridge did not seem as appealing as the phone call they looked forward to each evening. Kate was, however, curious about the appointment she had made to see Buck while he was in Utrecht .

As she told Jake about the meeting, she could sense him pull away from the conversation.

"Are you upset about my seeing Buck after my presentation tomorrow?"

"Well yeah, I guess it just…"

"Jake there is no need to worry about Buck! He's just a friend who helped me through a tough time."

"Love interest?" Jake queried.

Kate laughed, "Don't think I'm making light of your concern, but Buck would never be a love interest." She proceeded to describe Buck's age, appearance, and demeanor, and Jake immediately relaxed. What Kate didn't share was the latest email she had received from Buck.

To: KateW

From: BuckyM

Subject: Need to Meet

Kate, I know you are in Utrecht. Must meet with you. Be very careful. I am being watched and followed. Don't approach me on the street or in public. It's too dangerous! Meet me at the Café Orange Crown. Tomorrow, Tuesday the 24th 3:15 pm sharp. Back table across from the bar.

Kate this is very dangerous! Wait until I come to you. Don't wave or do anything until I come to your table!

Buck

It sounded as if Buck was in some sort of trouble, and Kate had already decided to help him in any way she could. After all, he had been the only person she could talk to during the darkest time in her life. His current problem obviously had to do with Lansdun, but she could not imagine what "danger" could be involved. Kate was concerned about the tone of the email but still felt Buck was being a tad overdramatic, and decided to not mention it to Jake.

Chapter 9
Tuesday, Utrecht, The Netherlands

Kate woke up early with three things on her mind. First, the meeting this morning at 8am sharp, with Kate as the first presenter. Next, the appointment with Buck at the café on Kanaalstraat and then the best part, seeing Jake the next day in Leiden.

Once she finished the presentation, the rest of her day passed quickly. The Utrecht group was impressed with the accomplishments of Kate and her team in Texas, and she accepted their compliments graciously. After a short lunch and a goodbye to her Dutch colleagues, she returned to her room. Originally she had planned a tour of the Utrecht research facility and a final dinner with the Dutch team, but Buck's email changed her plans. She was anxious to get their meeting behind her so she could talk with Jake on the phone.

Kate took a taxi across town to Old Utrecht, arrived at the café about 3 pm, and walked in to find the table Buck had referenced in his email. Unfortunately, it was occupied. The party quickly finished, though, and Kate took her place in the corner seat of the table with a perfect view of the busy cobblestone street outside.

Kate studied the little café, pleased that Buck had chosen a table inside in the corner of the café. Outside was a row of tables, an ideal place to meet and sit on a bright sunny day, but today was cool, and overcast with drizzling rain. The café fronted the narrow yet very busy street, Kanaalstraat, that connected to another road, creating a small wedge island of concrete to guide the traffic. As quaint and tranquil as this area of town seemed, Kate was amazed at how fast traffic passed by on the street.

As she waited for Buck, she ordered a Heineken on tap and sat back to enjoy the atmosphere of the café. She savored the flavor of the national beer and noticed how much better it tasted than the bottles back home. Kate thought about Buck's email and wondered what he had to share and how it would involve her.

Three-fifteen arrived with no Buck. Typical of Buck, late as always. A minute later she saw him hurrying down the sidewalk of the road that joined Kanaalstraat. He looked to be in a hurry, nervous, paranoid and disheveled. He glanced around in every direction as if being followed. Kate watched in horror as a black Mercedes with tinted windows suddenly jumped the curb and plowed into Buck. The impact of the collision sent him flying about 30 feet into the air. As he landed, Kate knew instantly Buck was dead.

She sat momentarily stunned, but seconds later jumped up. Before she had taken two steps, another black Mercedes pulled up. Two men scrambled out, picked up Buck's body and threw it into the trunk of the first car, which sped off. The second car pulled into the alley beside the café. The driver stepped out to join the two men, now walking casually along the same sidewalk where Buck had been walking. She recognized one of the three men from a picture in the Lansdun International Security Team presentation she had seen at the meeting. Her heart seemed to stop. This was no accident.

The men conferred for a moment, then split up and appeared to be looking for something or someone. Immediately, Kate realized that someone was very likely to be the person Buck was coming to meet. Kate took a step back toward her table, spied the back door of the café and slipped out.

Kate entered the alley and almost ran into the black Mercedes. She hurried down the alley way that soon emptied into a large brick plaza in front of an ancient cathedral. She slipped into the Dutch Reformed

Church, hoping for a place to hide while she tried to figure out what to do next.

As she sat in the centuries-old wooden pew, Kate contemplated her situation. I should contact the authorities.. There's no body. They'd think I was nuts. Call someone at Lansdun? But that's what Buck had labeled as 'dangerous'. The American Embassy? Kate felt herself quickly running out of options when Jake popped into her mind. He'll know what to do!

Kate looked around to see if she had been followed, then quickly left the church, grabbed a cab and returned to her hotel. On the way back, the taxi passed the café and there was no sign of the black Mercedes. At the hotel she stopped at the front desk to check out, then went up to her room to finish packing. Before leaving the hotel she left a message for her colleagues with the concierge that she would not be joining them for dinner. The porter put her bags into the taxi, and as the cab drove away, she was relieved not to see a black Mercedes anywhere in sight. On the way to the train station, she sat in the middle of the back seat, as far from the windows as possible.

Chapter 10
Tuesday Evening Kurhaus Hotel

Jake's last meeting ended at about 6:30 pm. As he made his way through the front lobby filled with people, he turned as he heard his name barely audible over the crowd.

"Jake! Jake!"

He turned and saw Kate. Excited but puzzled to see her in the lobby of the Kurhaus hotel in Scheveningen, he hurried to where she stood just inside the giant revolving doors. "Kate, what a surprise! What are you doing here? I thought you were coming tomorrow." Then he saw the tears in her eyes.

"Jake, I didn't know what to do. It was so horrible, I had to leave in a hurry, he was hit by a car, he--"

Jake interrupted, "Kate, calm down, sit right here! I'll be back in a second and I want to know all about it, stay right here!" Gratefully, Kate sank into a chair in the lobby, tears rolling down her face.

Jake grabbed Kate's suitcase and took it over to the bellman and with a 20 Euro bill asked the man to take the bag up to his room. Minutes later, Jake and Kate were sitting in the bar in a quiet booth away from the crowd and Kate told her story. In the three hours since the tragedy, Kate had calmed down enough to be able to describe every detail. After relating the horror of her afternoon, she put her head in her hands and wept again. "Jake I just don't know what to do next. I don't know who I can trust"

Jake slid over closer to her in the round booth and brought her close to his body in a hug. "Right now we do nothing except get you some food and some rest, then we'll talk about our options." Kate nodded silently and they stood up to leave the bar as Jake settled the tab by charging it to his room. Arm in arm they moved toward the elevator.

"What did you do with my bags?" Kate asked.

"Your bags are already in my room."

Kate turned and smiled with a look that was somewhat surprised as the elevator doors closed.

Once in the room, Kate took a shower and changed clothes, as if she could wash the afternoon clean. While she was in the bathroom, Jake called room service, then changed clothes, donning his favorite blue jeans, golf shirt, and deck shoes. It was the first time since he arrived in Holland that he was finally able to relax. He had looked forward to Kate's arrival, and even though she had come with some disturbing "baggage," he was very glad to see her. He heard the bathroom door open and Kate appeared wearing a t-shirt, blue jeans and sandals and toweling her hair. She apologized for her lack of makeup, but Jake was intrigued with her beauty and the tone of her skin. He always knew she would look just as beautiful without makeup. He walked over and took her in his arms. "You're even more beautiful than I remembered!" He pulled her close and kissed her. "I am here to help you Kate."

A knock on the door caused them both to jump apart. "Room Service."

"Room service," they both repeated, then laughed.

The waiter brought in their meal on a cart with metal lids covering the food. Jake directed him to put it in the corner of the large room. The waiter expanded the cart to a small table, then set it and lit candles. "Shall I open the wine, sir?" he asked.

"No, that will be all. Thank you," Jake replied and escorted the waiter to the door with a large tip.

Kate smiled, "Only you could find a way to give a horrible day a perfect ending."

"Tonight we relax. Tomorrow we try to figure it all out. So let's enjoy the evening. Bon Appetit!" Jake crossed the room to pull a chair up to the table for Kate.

"If I had known this was such a fancy restaurant, I would have dressed up."

"Trust me, you look just fine."

Kate lifted the lids of the covered dishes. "All my favorites!" she exclaimed. "How did you know?"

Jake shrugged "Feeling lucky tonight," he joked.

They ate steaks and salmon, drank wine, and laughed a lot. Jake was pleased that he was able to keep Kate's mind off what she had witnessed earlier but knew she was anxious to sort out. He would ultimately have to let her talk it out. He selfishly admitted to himself that he wanted to prolong that as long as possible.

"You were telling me about your first car . . ." Jake prompted.

"My grandmother's 1979 Town Car," she groaned. "I never volunteered to drive, but somehow we would all end up going in the "Gray Whale.""

Though they lingered over the cheesecake as long as possible, the dinner was over too soon. Jake piled up the dishes and rolled the cart out into the hall while Kate moved the chairs back in front of the window. When Jake returned from the hall, she was lying on the bed and patted the mattress next to her, calling Jake to her side. When he joined her, she leaned in and kissed him before saying softly, "Thank you for rescuing me today." Jake returned her kiss, held her close and felt the tension she carried.

As he waited for Kate to talk about Buck, Jake held her and was surprised when she simply drifted off to sleep. He lay awake for about an hour trying make sense of the story from the information Kate had given him. He got up carefully, went into the bathroom and brushed his teeth. As he walked back to the bed he noticed the room had growing colder, so he pulled up the comforter to cover both of them as he climbed back into bed next to her.

As he slept, he dreamed of Kate and the time they would have together over the next few days.. It surprised him how being next to Kate felt so natural, so right.

In the middle of the night Jake stirred as he felt Kate leave the bed. He soon was completely awakened as Kate returned and leaned over to kiss him on the cheek. He turned to return the kiss, reaching out to hug her and the surprise of touching her bare skin. He slid his hand across her back and down below her waist and felt her completely nude body. As he pulled her closer, she whispered a command, "Get undressed." Jake tried to respond and she put her hand over his mouth and said again, "Get undressed." Jake quickly removed his clothes and slid back under the comforter to be warmed by the heat of her body. He reached out and felt every detail of her body, memorizing each curve of her soft skin, all the time kissing her passionately. Before they lost control, Kate pulled Jake on top of her, releasing feelings and emotions that both of them had long locked away.

The next morning they awoke in each other's arms as the sun peaked in though the closed blinds. Jake leaned over and kissed Kate.

She opened her eyes. "Good morning, Dr. Patterson. I appreciate you giving me some space last night. I really needed the rest."

"Glad to oblige."

Kate sat up letting the sheet fall, unembarrassed, and asked, "What now?"

"I have an idea."

"I bet you do," Kate smiled, "But we really need to deal with my crisis, remember!"

"Well, you better get dressed or I won't be able to hear you talk.

Jake put off his desires and got up to get ready for the day. After each showered and dressed comfortably for travel, they packed their bags and got ready to leave for Leiden.

Aboard the train for the 20 minute ride to Leiden, Jake went over with Kate the details of her day yesterday. As Kate finished telling about her quick departure to the train station in Utrecht, he asked, "Are you sure you weren't followed?"

"Positive. I never told anyone that I had a meeting with Buck, or that he had been emailing me."

Jake, taken aback, looked a little concerned that this was the first time she had mentioned the email contact. But then reminded himself that this whole situation had unfolded quickly, and he and Kate had had limited communication. After all, the plane ride was just a few days ago.

Kate frowned. "I was going to tell you about the emails, but I was never sure if I needed to take them seriously. Buck was so dramatic."

"I understand, Kate. But now I think we have to consider everything to be serious."

She nodded, and told him about all the emails, including the last one from Buck insisting they meet. "It sounded urgent. Like he really needed to show me or tell me something."

"Obviously, somebody knew he had something to tell."

They both agreed nothing could be done about it at the moment. Here they were in a foreign country, with a story that no one would believe. A murder. No body. Motive unknown.

As the train pulled up to the Leiden Central Station, the door opened and Kate and Jake stepped out into a warm and sunny, spring day. Pulling their bags, they made their way out into the plaza in front of the train station.

Jake turned and spread his arms wide. "Here it is, Leiden! What do you think of my home away from home so far?"

Kate grinned. "I love it! Reminds me of my childhood home. It looks something like Beacon Hill back in Boston."

As they headed toward town from the train station, the plaza narrowed into a shop-lined street and their wheeled luggage clacked on the cobblestones. Rows of brick buildings consisted mainly of ground floor shop fronts with apartment homes above. They passed by familiar businesses such as grocery stores, a bank and hair salon, all contained within the quaint Dutch structures.

Kate tugged on his sleeve. "Hardly anyone walks around here. They're all on bicycles."

Just past a Chinese restaurant, Jake turned down an alley. "This way. Come on, Oma's waiting."

"We can walk to your grandparent's house? I thought we'd get to ride a Dutch bus!"

"Not today." Jake led her down the alley and out onto a back street. They crossed and made their way a couple of blocks to another street. As they walked down the sidewalk, Kate recognized the street to be strictly residential with beautiful family homes. The entrance to each home began with a small brick wall and a tiny yard. The homes were well kept but obviously showing some age as some of the homes were several hundred years old. After they passed several larger homes, Jake turned into one of the courtyards.

"Here we are. This is where I spent most of my summers as a boy."

"But, this is a hotel. Where is your grandparent's home?"

"Hotel Leiden! This is their home. I guess I never got to the part where Oma and Opa turned the house into a bed and breakfast hotel after he retired. Money got a little tight and they considered selling the old place before they got the idea to start a business. With no family around Leiden anymore, Oma found a way to use her gift of hospitality. It may be a hotel, but when I come, it's Grandma's house, as it always was. Oma never rents any rooms out when I tell her I'm coming to visit. She insists on it being a home for my visit, and there's plenty of room for you."

As they neared the front porch, the door swung open with the sound of a rattling bell, and Oma burst through the door yelling, "Jakob, Jakob! Come see me, my engeltje. It has been so long. Too long. Do come inside. When you called to tell us you were bringing a friend, you didn't tell me she was so beautiful. Come this way both of you. We must get some coffee and talk."

Jake smiled as he looked at Kate. She looked bewildered by the whirlwind caused by the little lady known as Oma. "She's not what I expected to see. Not really the old grandmotherly type," she whispered.

"Yes, Oma's always been full of energy. She is one special grandma."

"I think I'm going to like it here."

They walked up the steps together with Oma to meet Opa, still standing in the open doorway. Jake led Kate into the living area. A grand old fireplace trimmed with antique Blue Delft tiles depicting the various occupations of old Leiden dominated the room. Jake and Kate sat on a couch in front of the fireplace, sipping strong Dutch coffee. The brick of the hearth extended out onto the floor where one could easily stand near the warmth. However, there was no fire today, only the warmth of the reunion of Jake and his grandparents.

After a visit and a small lunch, Jake and Kate followed Oma up the stairs to their rooms on the third floor. Jake would be in his usual suite, and Kate in the smaller room next door. After opening the rooms Oma walked toward the stairs and turned to speak before going down.

"Jake, you and Kate have the whole floor to yourselves. I will just shut this door at the top of the stairs so you can have privacy. Dinner is at 7 pm tonight. You might want to tour the town this evening and see how they are setting up for the music festival that begins tomorrow night. Let me know if you need anything" Oma quickly stepped back and shut the door, leaving Jake and Kate all alone.

"Jake, this is wonderful. Your grandparents are precious. Thanks so much for bringing me here. I know this will be like therapy for me."

"Okay, but I was hoping it would be fun, too."

"I'm sure it will be. What's this about a music festival?"

"If we're lucky we'll get a glimpse. The whole town explodes with people and I can guarantee you've never been to anything like it. It's like a three day party. I had forgotten it was this weekend."

"Sounds great. I just need a few minutes to freshen up."

Jake and Kate made their way down the steep, narrow stairs to the first floor. Jake led her through the kitchen and announced their departure to his grandmother. The couple slipped out the back door and stopped in front of two bicycles.

"Bikes? I haven't ridden a bike in years. I don't know, Jake."

"This is how we get around in Leiden." He grinned then winked at her. "It'll be fun."

They spent the rest of the afternoon riding through Leiden. Kate was mesmerized at the homey atmosphere of the town. The streets followed the canals, and buildings lined the streets up to complete the picture. The town looked so European, beautiful yet it reminded her of Utrecht and Buck's death. She pushed those thoughts aside and tried to focus on the beauty of Leiden. As they took in the sights, time passed very quickly and before they knew it dusk was beginning to settle upon the busy little Dutch town. Kate and Jake made their way back to his grandparent's house where Oma was waiting. She greeted them at the door and instructed them to get ready for dinner.

"I've been cooking all afternoon. Hurry up, you two. I know you must be hungry."

During dinner Opa left the table and returned with an envelope. "Jake, we got tickets for you at the Keukenhof for tomorrow. Here are two round trip train tickets and two tickets to the park. Your Oma and I know how much you love to visit there. This is our little gift to you."

Jake got up from the table and walked around to embrace his grandparents. "Dank u wel, Oma and Opa! I had just promised Kate on the plane that we would try to visit the Keukenhof."

With dinner over, Kate and Jake retired to their rooms. Kate quickly changed to get ready for bed. As soon as she finished she heard a knock at the door.

"Come in," she called out knowing it had to be Jake.

He entered, talking. "You know this room is very special. Lauren and I stayed in here when we visited as kids. My parents always got the bigger room I'm in." He walked to the window and looked out into city lights.

"We used to sit here and try to count the different roof tops we could see." He paused and smiled as he reminisced. "If you're not too tired come over to my room. There's a nice sitting area in front of the window. We can talk for a while."

In a few minutes Kate joined Jake in his room. Jake was at the window, cracking it a bit to let in the fresh breeze. He turned and embraced her with a kiss before leading her to the couch where they held each other and talked. After a while he excused himself to get ready for bed and Kate climbed between the sheets to wait. Jake turned off the lights, slipped under the covers and embraced her. They fell asleep holding each other and woke to soft rays of morning sun slashing through the blinds.

As they got ready for their trip to the Keukenhof, they smelled fresh coffee and Dutch pastries that Oma prepared downstairs. Jake smiled, "My Oma …" Quickly they finished getting ready and made their way downstairs for breakfast.

Kate and Jake took the train to Leise, a town in the northwestern part of the Netherlands, home to the famous Keukenhof Gardens. Since a child, Jake had enjoyed visiting the world's largest flower garden. He could probably only name about 20 of the 7,000,000 varieties, but he loved looking at all of them. The bright sunshine lit up the entrance sign and he held out his hand to Kate. She hugged her sweater closer to ward off the cool breeze from the North Sea, smiled and took his hand. Her palm felt soft and warm and right against his. He hoped the gardens would take Kate far away from the events she witnessed at Utrecht.

Kate was immediately attracted to the bursts of color as they entered the park. She silently admonished herself, "I need to let go of Buck. How can I allow myself any negative thought when surrounded by this beauty?"

Over the next three hours, Jake showed Kate every inch of the gardens, and she knew he was doing his best to keep her from thinking about Buck. They stopped for lunch at one of the outdoor cafe's that overlooked a spectacular splash of color.

"I can't believe Buck's gone, Jake. One minute he's his nerdy self, racing to see me and the next minute he's dead. Why would anyone kill him?"

Jake held her hand and listened.

She calmed as she talked. By the time she'd finished venting, she realized how safe Jake made her feel. She pulled her chair next to his and leaned her head on his shoulder. He kissed her earlobe, then they sat and looked out at the flowers as the waiter cleared their table.

His hand on her chin, he turned her face toward him. "Come on, there's one more place I want to show you. My favorite place."

Kate hurried to keep up with his quickening pace. He seemed filled with the excitement of an 8 year old, and she ran to keep up.

"Come on Kate, you will not believe this."

He stopped at a turn in the walkway and waited for her to catch up. He grabbed her hand and pulled her around the bend.

Kate stopped and sucked in a breath at the beauty before them. Large trees with bursts of color between them framed a pond. Flowers grew on slopes that rose up and away from the water's edge. Their perfect position around the pond and amazing splash of bright colors of blue, yellow, red, and white that filled the space in between the trees gave the effect of an impressionistic painting.

Jake, still holding her hand led her to a bench beside the water. Just as Kate began to release all her thoughts about Buck's death, Jake broke the tranquility. "Kate, what do you think about us going back to Utrecht, to look around and check out the scene of the crime?"

"What do you mean, uh, ok, maybe, that's not a bad idea."

"I think you need some closure. What you saw back in Utrecht is really haunting you. Maybe going back together, we'll get some answers."

"Okay," said Kate hesitantly, "But we'll need to be very careful."

Decision made, Kate and Jake left the Keukenhof and returned to Leiden. If they were going to go to Utrecht in the morning, they had a lot of planning to do. At the station, Jake picked up a schedule for departures to Utrecht.

Chapter 11
Friday – Trip to Utrecht

The next morning they got up for an early start, and both were dressed and ready to go by 5:30 am. They walked down the stairs quietly, hoping not to wake anyone, but as they reached the last landing before the lobby, Kate and Jake heard Oma's voice.

"Jake, I know you are going on a trip today and I don't want you to go away without a meal. I have some brodjekaas and fruit for you." The cheese sandwiches that Oma made were a favorite of Jake's. She also prepared a bag with extra cheese, ham, and a baguette. She handed them each a bottle of water, then with hugs and kisses, sent them on to the train station. Jake knew they there was no chance they could have left the house undetected, and thought fondly of Oma's familiar departure routine.

They boarded the train at Leiden Central Station and selected window seats facing each other. As the train pulled out of the station, Jake was able to point out the sights along the way and at the same time explain some of the nuances of Dutch culture.

"Kate, have you heard the saying 'God made the world, but the Dutch made Holland'?"

"Yes, but I don't really know what that means."

"Holland has been plagued with flooding. Since about 25% of the country is below sea level, the land is filled with dams and dikes designed to keep the North Sea at bay. Something like 400,000 acres of land have been reclaimed from the sea."

"The little boy who plugged the dike and saved the country!"

"You heard my story? I had to do that one year when I came to visit Oma and Opa. There's a statue of me in Volendam"

"You goofball!" Kate laughed.

"You got me. But everything else was on the level. I'm especially impressed by the canal system that keeps the land dry. Originally the windmills used the wind off the North Sea to help pump the water where it's wanted, but now modern pumping stations work night and day to keep the reclaimed land dry."

Up until the train began to slow as it entered the station, Jake shared what he knew about the people and places of the Netherlands. Kate and Jake grabbed their stuff and waited for the doors to open. Outside the station, they found the large map of the town hanging in a frame near the posted bus schedules .

"Look, Jake, the cafe is somewhere right over here in Old Utrecht, by city hall and there's the church that I ran to,", Kate said as she pointed on the map.

"Okay, let's find a cab."

A ten minute cab ride and four Euros got them to the large cathedral. They stood on the sidewalk as Kate looked around. " Nothing looks familiar except the church. I guess I was just too frazzled. Wait! I just remembered, I picked up a book of matches from the Café. It's here somewhere in my purse. Yes, here it is, the address is right on the back."

Café D'Orange Crown

419 East Canal Street

Utrecht

"I have no idea which way to go but I know it's within walking distance from here. If only I could remember where the alley way is."

"Wait a minute I have an idea. Stay here." Jake crossed the street into a Beninhoff. After just a few minutes he returned with a map of old Utrecht. "I asked about the café and the lady pointed it out on the map. He unfolded the map. "Here it is. Can you figure out the route?"

Kate studied the location of the Café and found where a back door would come out. After a minute or two she pointed across the street. "There, that's the little alley way."

Hand in hand, they walked slowly across the street and into the alleyway. What had seemed like a long distance to Kate during her frantic escape turned out to be in actuality only three short blocks. The thought of running such a short distance from the café gave her a chill as she realized how narrow an escape it had been.

As they walked into the street behind the café, Kate could not even recognize the door she had come out of, so they decided to walk around the block. As they turned the corner, Kate looked down the street and saw the sidewalk tables.

"I don't want to go back there." She squeezed his hand. "How about the café across the street?"

They crossed at the intersection. Inside, the smell of fresh bread greeted them. At their request, a waiter took them to one of the outside tables, giving them a clear Vantage point of the crime scene.

"It would have been too spooky to go inside and show you the table, I feel much safer here. We still have a clear view of Café D'Orange Crown."

"Tell me again what you saw."

Kate described in detail where Buck was when he was hit and where the cars parked to load his body.

"See, there's a black tire mark on the curb. And there right by that sign is where Buck landed."

As he listened, Jake felt sure others had seen what happened.

After a lunch of chicken satay and pommefrites, the waitress asked in English, "Would you like anything else?"

Jake responded in Dutch, "Geen dank u."

"U bent Nederlands?" She switched from English to Dutch. "Ikdacht, was u Amerikaans."

Jake answered in Dutch, "Actually I'm American, my mother is Dutch and my grandparents live in Leiden."

"You are very fluent, no accent at all."

"Thank you, I take pride in my Dutch. Do you know Leiden?"

"Why, yes, as a matter of fact I am studying in Leiden. This spring I had to take off to care for my mother. She is much better now and I can't wait to get back. Leiden feels more like home to me than Utrecht."

Jake hoped this young waitress could shed some light on the accident, so he changed the conversation. "Seems like it's slow around here today, such a beautiful day and all."

"This time of day it is usually slow. It really picks up at night time. Really pretty dull around except for several days ago."

"Really? What happened?"

"Someone was hit by a car. I saw it. No one here believes me. I was cleaning up a table by the window there." She turned and pointed inside. "A man was run over by a black Mercedes. Another car pulled up behind it, two men picked up the man, and they were gone. It happened so fast. I ran and called the police. They came by and interviewed me, went out to look at the area I described and then came back to say they didn't find anything. They even questioned if I was telling the truth. So of course no one here believes me. I almost lost my job over it. Please don't say anything to my boss or anyone here I told you that story or I could really lose my job." After a long sigh, "I am so ready to get back to Leiden."

Jake thanked the waitress and settled the bill. He looked at Kate and said, "Let's go."

"Jake, wait a minute! You just had a two minute conversation with that girl. I know it was about Buck, what did she say? What did she see?

"Kate, let's leave quietly and I'll tell you outside," he whispered.

As soon as they left the Café, Jake and Kate crossed the street and hurried past the Café D'Orange Crown.

At the corner, she stopped him. "Jake, what were you talking about?"

"She saw the whole thing and described it just as you did. Called the police and everything!"

"What did the police do?"

"Nothing, they didn't believe her. Everyone including her coworkers think she made it all up. This is just so bizarre."

Jake unfolded the map to find the best way back to the station. After discovering they were only about 10 blocks away, he insisted on walking, so they could have time to think.

After a couple of blocks, Jake stopped again to look at the map. "There." He pointed to the intersection ahead. "We need to cross there." As he glanced back at Kate, something caught his eye. "No, it couldn't be!" He moved past Kate as if she wasn't there in the opposite direction he had just pointed.

"Jake, where are you going? You just said we need to go the other way. Jake, wait!" She ran to catch up with him.

He stopped and stared at a small office door with the words, Jan Metler, Tandarts. "There it is!"

"What?"

"This office."

"What does Tandarts mean?"

"Literal translation is 'tooth doctor'. This is a dental office. No this is the dental office. The logo, look at the sign, that symbol! This is too bizarre. It must somehow all be connected."

"Jake, what on earth are you talking about?"

"Kate, last week my friend Paul Baker, the Triumph Chief of Police, had me over at the morgue to look at a murder victim. The coroner showed me an x-ray with that symbol on it. Just before I left for this trip I had a patient, a Dutch man, with that Tooth Doctor sign on his tooth."

"What?"

"The victim and my patient were both in their mid 20s. Both had a crown with that symbol. The symbol was not visible when you looked at the tooth. Only on an x-ray. The corpse and my patient were somehow connected to this sign, this dental office."

"What does this have to do with Buck's death?"

"I'm not sure but I do know my patient was in town to interview with Lansdun. They don't know the identification of the man in the morgue, but both men have to have some connection."

"Jake, let's get out of here and head back to Leiden. This is getting scary."

They hurried to the train station. During the 50 minute ride back to Leiden, Jake went over the details of both x-rays. The coincidence of both men with the same letters on a crown that showed up only on an x-ray was very strange.

"Why would anyone need to have a logo show up on an x-ray only?" Kate asked.

"I don't know. I've never seen anything like this before. Somebody went to a lot of trouble to make a porcelain crown with a special marking."

"Hidden to everyone except by x-ray? Why take the chance it would be seen by another dentist?"

"The only thing I can think of is that it was meant to mark that crown for identification. Kate, these patients have to be connected to Buck. Two men in Triumph, Texas possibly connected to Lansdun. All these things are connected to a Dutch dentist."

"I still don't see a connection to Buck. I didn't realize we had any men coming over from Utrecht for interviews. Get me the name of your patient when we get home and I'll try to find out more. I do have access to Lansdun's personnel files. "

"Great idea. Maybe this lead will help us make some sense out of Buck's death."

Back in Leiden, Kate and Jake quickly changed then walked to the large plaza down by the canal to the stages set up for the festival. The main stage was set in the middle of the canal very close to the Leiden University Campus. Vendors selling their wares filled every empty spot on the street. People roamed everywhere. Beer, dancing, and lively music filled the town of Leiden and before they knew it, it was time to head back to Oma's house once again. Jake reminded Kate that this was only the first night of the party. It would get crazier and busier before it ended in two days. But tomorrow would be their last day in Leiden, tomorrow they would rest and prepare for an early start on Saturday morning. And something was amiss at Lansdun International.

Chapter 12
Saturday

Early the next morning, Oma greeted them with a large breakfast of eggs, ham, cheese and various kinds of fruit. The smell of coffee blended with the aroma of the breakfast and gave Kate the feeling that she would truly miss the experience she had had in Leiden. Jake was one lucky guy to have family like this to support him. With breakfast out of the way, minutes passed quickly and it was time to leave for Schiphol airport. Oma and Opa insisted on driving them to the airport instead of allowing them to take the train as they had planned.

"Jake, you and Kate have been such wonderful guests, we want to spend every minute we can with you. Kate, it has been such a gift to meet you and I know we will see much more of you in the future," she said with a wink and a small grin. With that remark Jake knew Kate was accepted to be part of the family. Oma's approval of Kate carried a lot of weight with Jake.

Just then Opa came in the back door and announced it was time to leave. "Jake, Kate, we need to be leaving if we are going to get there for Jake's two hour window before the flight.

Kate turned and looked at Jake with a puzzled expression. Jake responded, "I have a little problem with being early with everything. It's almost an obsession."

"Almost!" Opa replied, "Ha!, I would say much more than an obsession." He followed with a laugh.

"Opa, you're not helping me make a good impression here on Kate."

"Seems like she already knows everything about you," he said as he grinned.

"Okay, jongens, we need to get in the car. Time to go," Oma ordered.

Everyone obeyed and the car was quickly loaded and the group made their way up the highway to Schiphol airport. Hugs and kisses were plentiful at the airport. After placing their luggage on the curb, Kate and Jake stood arm in arm as they waved goodbye to Jake's grandparents. When the car drove out of sight, they hurried into the airport to find the Continental Airline terminal. With First Class tickets in hand they followed the line snaking to the check in desk. They placed their bags on the scale and watched as the bags were tagged, loaded onto the conveyor belt, only to disappear down a hidden ramp to where they would be loaded onto the plane.

"Continental Flight 47, seats 3a and 3b, First Class, we are all set to leave, Kate."

"Jake, I'm not sure I want to go back to the mess that may be waiting for us back home."

"What do you mean, the mess?" He worried she was talking about them.

"Buck."

"Well, we have almost 11 hours to figure out what we'll do when we get home. Come on, let's get to the gate."

"Wait, first I need to get some souvenirs for your nieces." Kate quickly ran into a store as Jake waited outside watching their carryon bags directly across from the KLM counter. He noticed the lines of people beginning to check in for KLM's Houston flight leaving at 3:30 pm.

Kate appeared out of the store with a bag full of trinkets and two wrapped boxes. "Look what I got Jake!" Before she could get another word out, she gasped, and stepped back into the store. "Jake, come here!"

Surprised at her tone, Jake quickly moved back into the store.

"Look," she whispered, "there in the line in front of the KLM counter, the two men in light colored suits. Those are two of the men who were there when Buck was killed. And the second one is the one I recognized from the security briefing when I was at the Lansdun headquarters. Are they going to Houston?"

"Sure looks that way Kate. Let's get to our gate. It's in a whole different area than KLM so we won't have to see them in the airport before we leave."

"Good, I don't think I could deal with it if they recognized me. But I guess we need to be prepared that they will be in Triumph about the same time we get there. I wonder what they're up to."

"We'll find out soon enough. Let's go this way. They won't spot us down this corridor. There, over there, is the security for the terminal D area."

Kate and Jake used the time on the flight wisely to work on a strategy of how they would probe further into Buck's death and the possible connection between the man in the morgue and Jake's patient with the strange inscription on his crown.

"Kate, how much access do you have to the computer main frame at Lansdun in Triumph?"

"Well, pretty much everything. I do manage the department that oversees that. The only problem would be that I usually don't access it or have much to do with that department unless we have a problem. Security is pretty tight, but I might be able to do some snooping."

"Good, you begin there and try to find out if there is any traffic about Buck's death, him not showing up for work, or anything else peculiar. Did Buck have any relatives or family that you knew about?"

"I'm not sure. I can do some checking in the personnel files, there should be some sort of reference to that somewhere."

"Okay, so I'll try to find out more about the patients I saw and their x-rays. Now that I know what I may be looking for I'll try to make some sense of it all."

"Jake, thanks for helping me with this."

"My pleasure." Jake leaned over and kissed Kate playfully.

"Enough of all this serious stuff about Buck. Dinner should be coming soon." Jake pressed the call button. Moments later, they were enjoying a glass of wine together.

The rest of the trip proved uneventful except for some turbulence now and then. Tasty meals, good movies, but most of all intimate conversation occupied their time. Then with seats reclined and cabin lights dimmed, Jake and Kate drifted off to sleep.

They were awakened by the sound of the wheels dropping from the base of the plane as it got ready to land in Houston. A short taxi put the plane at the gate of the International Terminal at Houston Intercontinental Airport right on time at 5:45 pm.

The plan had been for Jake to be picked up by his sister at the airport, but Kate insisted on driving Jake to his sister's house so she could meet her. With bags in hand, they made their way to the parking garage and began to look for her car.

"There it is! The blue BMW, up there on the right!"

Jake followed as she hurried ahead of him, thinking that not only did he fall in love with a great girl, but also a girl with great taste in cars. "I must say, I love the car, Kate. I had a similar one when I lived in Houston years ago, but sold it to get a country Cadillac, you know an SUV."

"Oh, it's just a car, I could really drive anything, but this one was nice and has a very smooth ride." They loaded their bags in the trunk and quickly exited the garage for the ride north to his sister's house. Jake had called her from the airport and as usual the twins were there waiting to greet him as they drove up.

"Uncle Jake, Uncle Jake, what did you bring us?" Ashley and Marley rushed from the porch toward the car.

"Girls, I brought you both a very special present. Her name is Kate."

"Ah, Uncle Jake," Marley yelled, "We mean what gift did you bring us?"

"Yeah, Uncle Jake," Ashley joined in.

Jake walked around to the back of the car and opened the trunk. He reached in and pulled out two wrapped boxes. "I looked long and hard for something very special and I found you these," he said, with a wink at Kate. He watched as the girls tore open their gifts.

Marley let out a scream, "Uncle Jake, it's so cute, I've always wanted one of these. A little Dutch girl doll with wooden shoes. Did grandma dress like this when she was a girl back in Holland?"

"A twin, look a twin," Ashley yelled, "Just like Marley's! Thanks Uncle Jake."

Lauren walked out of the house to greet Jake and Kate and as the screen door shut behind her, the girls turned and ran to their mother to show her the dolls. "Mom, Mom, look what Uncle Jake brought us."

"Oh girls, they're so beautiful. They look just like you do."

"Yeah," they screamed in unison, "We're going to go play, bye Uncle Jake, bye Miss Kate".

"Lauren, let me introduce a very special lady, this is Kate."

Lauren walked up to the couple and said, "Kate, I am so pleased to meet you. I feel like I already know you, I just got off the phone with Oma and she is very impressed with you."

"Lauren, your girls are so beautiful, they're adorable."

"Well, thanks, but I'm afraid you just saw them at their best. They sure love their Uncle Jake. Come inside, let's visit awhile."

Jake, Kate and Lauren drank iced tea on the screened porch as the girls played with their new dolls. The visit was short since Kate and Jake were tired from the long plane ride, but plans were made for the Page family to come up to Triumph and visit the house at the lake.

"Kate, why don't you take the lead and I'll follow you to your house. Don't drive too fast in that fancy car of yours."

"Don't worry I won't let you out of my sight."

As they drove away from the house, the girls stood in the front yard waving. Within minutes Jake and Kate were on Hwy 59 heading north to Triumph, both glad to be headed home and excited about what their new life together would bring.

Kate pulled onto a tree lined street, slowed and turned right into a driveway and stopped just in front of the sidewalk leading to the porch. Jake pulled in right behind her, then hurried to help her with her bags.

"Wait, first I need a hug. Do you realize we have not been apart from each other that long since we went to Leiden?"

Jake pulled her into his arms and followed the hug with a kiss. After letting her go he leaned in and removed the remaining bags from Kate's trunk. "Let me put my bags in my car, then I will be back to help with yours."

She grabbed him by the hand and led him inside. Right away he noticed a real warmth and comfort to the house, a confirmation that Kate was the right girl for him. She pointed to the couch by the fireplace, as he set the bags down by the door, then said, "Have a seat, I'm going to get more comfortable. If you want some wine there's a bottle of Pinot Noir on the counter, help yourself. The glasses are in the cabinet." Kate disappeared down a hall.

In the kitchen Jake found the bottle of wine and a corkscrew. He opened the cabinet and took out two red wine glasses and put them down on the counter next to the bottle. After opening the bottle he poured each glass and returned to the couch, in front of the stone fireplace, yet angled toward the lake. When Kate reappeared, she wore blue jeans and a t-shirt, looking very similar to way he had first seen her in Scheveningen after her shower. Simply amazing, he thought, what a beautiful woman Kate Williams is. I am a lucky man.

"Do you always have a bottle of wine waiting for guests, Kate?"

"No, silly, I called my housekeeper, Rita, from the airport. I knew she was probably just finishing up at the house and I asked her to put it out for us. Good idea, though, wasn't it?"

"Sitting here with you, snuggling on the couch with a nice glass of Pinot is pretty much my idea of heaven. Doesn't get much better that this."

"Oh, yes it does," Kate replied as she stood up, took his hand and led him down the hall to her room.

Chapter 12
Sunday in Triumph

Kate was wide awake after 4 hours. She was still on Leiden time. How in the world can Jake still sleep, she thought. She slipped out of bed, grabbed a robe, and headed to the living room. What do I do now? She eyed her bags by the front door, but decided the middle of the night was not a good time to tackle them. Maybe a glass of milk would help her sleep. As she entered the kitchen, she noticed a huge stack of mail. Well, that'll probably knock me out. She grabbed the basket and carried it to the couch.

A large DHL courier envelope sat in the middle of the stack. She quickly sorted through the mail on top of the DHL packet. Looking more closely, she noticed Buck's name in the corner. It had been date-stamped the day they were to meet and the return address was Utrecht.

She opened the package and inside were two envelopes: one large and one small. On the smaller envelope were the words, "Open This First." Inside was a note from Buck.

Kate,

If you have received this package then I am probably no longer alive. Kate, just recently I uncovered something that has put me in danger. I discovered that cell samples are indeed being smuggled into the Lansdun facility in Texas. I still don't know how they are being brought in but as I said before it is in very minute quantities. Observing in the lab, I noticed that the specimens that we were working with replicated very fast, and very shortly after arriving we had an ample supply of the cells. I never had a chance to know what the cells are used for but I do know that they are very aggressive in their general nature.

Secondly, I did discover where the cells were coming from. Apparently there is a joint US/Dutch project doing research on a certain type of military application. The information I have uncovered is that the material we have been using is stolen from that project going on in Utrecht. The weird thing that I haven't figured out is that the material must be kept at human body temperature and in a dark moist environment, I can't figure out how they're shipping it. Nothing comes into the lab with any kind of special packaging.

The bigger envelope has pictures in it of the specimens in question as well as copies of a file that I was able to look through from the lab. The file has receipts, invoices, travel costs, tickets and anything else one might need to move back and forth between two countries.

The other key thing I found out is that there is some connection to the Lansdun Security Vice President as well as the Special Projects Coordinator. It appears that the Special Projects Coordinator is behind the secret facility that I work in. I don't know what role the Security guy plays, but I gather it is in keeping the lid down on all of this. I am not sure if there are other players in the company higher up, but I wouldn't take a chance and share this with anyone.

One other thing Kate, I have found a back door into the lab's computer system. I was going to give you this in person but since I had to send this I can't help anymore. I have only accessed it once for a brief time but had to get out before anyone discovered me. With your security clearance you should be able to snoop around undetected, but you will need the code for the back door. I have created a user name for you to use. At a Lansdun networked workstation type in the following:

http://LansdunInternational/spprg/Tr/micro/4647

Username: JCooper

Password: 8515

Be careful and erase all trace of you getting on the site. I know you know how from our conversations during our first few meetings.

Be careful, this is really big. There are powerful people behind this. Watch your back Kate. Sorry to involve you in this but you are the only person I can trust.

Your Friend,

Buck

Just as she finished reading the letter, Jake appeared in the living room dressed only in boxers. "Kate, you coming back to bed?"

"Come look at this. I found it in my mail"

He sat down next to Kate as she handed him the letter. After reading the letter, he examined the outer envelope and the larger unopened envelope.

"Looks like this was sent from Utrecht."

"Yeah. Look at the date, it was sent the day he was killed."

"What's in this other package?"

"Buck mentioned photos."

"Open it. Let's see what's in it." Jake moved everything off the small coffee table so they could spread out the contents.

"Most of this stuff is meaningless without some sort of reference," Kate said. "For example, this page has nothing but file names on it, most with either document or spreadsheets endings in the name. But where are the documents located?" Except for the photos, the rest of the documents were receipts for travel, hotel, and purchases that seemed totally unrelated.

"Maybe the photos will make things clearer."

Most seemed to be taken with the same camera and by an amateur, probably Buck. They couldn't see a pattern to the pictures, yet knew they must have some significance.

"Let's lay them out and see if we can make some sense of it all." He picked up a pad of paper and documented each one:

Glass Petri Dish with culture medium and cell growth

Microscopic view of individual cells or microorganisms

5 pictures inside the lab where Buck had worked at Lansdun in Texas

1 Picture of man appearing to be in his mid-fifties

Picture of the outside of a building – some sort of lab.

Picture of Lansdun International Security Badge - #6946

Small storefront or office, as if taken from a moving vehicle.

The last photo caught Jake's attention. Although the image was somewhat blurry and taken from a distance, Jake felt sure he knew what the photo had captured. "Kate, do you have a magnifying glass?"

She hurried to the living room and returned with a square shaped magnifying glass.

Jake held it over the photo, moving it side to side until he saw what he was looking for. "Right there." He pointed. "*Tandarts, dhr. J. B. Metler.* Somehow this office is connected to Buck's death."

Kate dumped out the last piece of paper left in the envelope, a list of 5 names each with a line drawn through the name.

"Look, Kate. The last two names on this list. One of them is my patient. The one with the symbol embedded in his porcelain crown. The other one might be the dead guy in the morgue. But how do Dr. Metler, Lansdun, my patient, and Buck all connect together? "

Kate picked up Buck's letter and looked over it again. "Maybe this is the answer," she said and pointed to the paragraph that referenced a back door to the lab's computer. "I need to get to the office to access this."

"I'm not sure about that, Kate. It is way too dangerous. We need to go to the police. We should call my friend Chief Baker in on this."

"And tell him what? That I saw someone killed in Utrecht? That I have a letter and a bunch of photos of random stuff? Or maybe you could tell them about your patient's crown," Kate suggested sarcastically. "I agree we eventually need to go to the police but we need more information. I have to try to get into the computer at work."

"I don't know. I already left a message for Paul about the patient I saw before I left. Maybe they figured out what that guy in the morgue was. Maybe he already found a connection."

"I'm going to the office today." Kate shrugged. "Usually early on a Sunday morning there are only a few people there. It'll be much easier to snoop around."

"Alright then I'll get more information at my office about my Dutch patient. Maybe there's something in his patient record or x-rays that will make this thing a little clearer."

Kate wiped her eyes and yawned. "It's 3 am. We have a full day ahead of us. Let's try to get some sleep." She grabbed his willing hand and led him back to the bedroom. She fell asleep with the warmth of his body cradling her from behind.

Chapter 13

They woke up at 5am and hurried to get dressed so they could go to their offices to deal with their respective tasks. As Jake began to dress in yesterday's clothes, Kate jumped out of bed, let her robe drop to the floor as she made her way into the bathroom to shower. Jake was still amazed at how each glimpse of her beauty was new every time he saw her. He finished getting dressed and moved into the living room so that he could once again look over the contents of Buck's package.

Kate joined him, wearing slacks with a short sleeve shirt. She gathered up Buck's package to take to the office.

"I don't think you should take that with you to Lansdun. Do you have any place here in the house where it would be safe?"

Kate thought for a minute and decided that the best place to hide it was in her collection of albums. She had been collecting old L.P.s since she was a teenager and had over 200 records. A record sleeve would be a perfect place to hide the documents. Kate and Jake decided on the sleeve of the Beatles White Album.

After they left her house, Kate followed Jake out of the neighborhood. At the main road leading toward town, they turned opposite directions. Kate turned left to drive the 10 miles to Lansdun, hoping she could access the computer records and gain entry to the back door of the lab's computer. Jake turned right, toward his office in town to check his office computer system for the record of the patient from Utrecht. They had agreed to be back at Kate's house by 7, so he had about an hour.

Jake pulled up in front of his office. He entered the front door and saw that things looked very much as if they had the day he had left on his trip. His staff had been cleaning and everything looked spic and span and ready for a busy schedule Monday morning. Jake walked back to his office and sat down, looked at his schedule and was relieved to see that Kim had booked him for only half a day. He assumed she remembered the last time he came back from a trip to Europe and how tired he was when he got back. Amazed that Kim remembered this small detail, he realized how good he had it here at the office with such an attentive staff. He turned on his computer and checked email to look for anything from Brennan. Nothing yet. Brennan must be stumped on this one. He knew the patient's first name was Peter, but the last name eluded him.

A computer search of patient first names soon turned up the record he was looking for. "Ah yes, Peter Meijer."

Jake left his office, walked up front to the patient records, and pulled the chart. Sure enough everything lined up just as he had thought. He wrote down the information so he could remember it for Kate.

From Utrecht.

Here for a job interview at Lansdun.

Toothache on a tooth just treated in The Netherlands.

A porcelain crown with a logo embedded in it seen only on an x-ray.

Patient of Dr. Jan Metler.

After copying the health history and patient notes, he re-filed the chart, then accessed the computer x-ray files of Peter and printed a copy showing the symbol on his crown. His mission complete, Jake left the office and returned to Kate's house to wait for her.

Kate arrived at Lansdun International, turned into the drive and slowed to approach the security gate. As she pulled next to the guardhouse, she held out her ID badge to gain admittance.

"Morning, Ms. Williams, what brings you to work this early," asked Brian Palmer, the weekend security guard.

"Hi, Brian, I've been out of town for about a week and have a lot of catching up to do. I hope to get a good head start."

"Didn't expect to see you today. Well, don't work too hard. You can't let a day like this one go to waste."

"Thanks Brian, I won't be long."

Brian waved Kate through the gate and she pulled into the lot to park in her reserved space. One of the perks of her job, she thought as she got out of the car and entered the building. Her ID badge was also her key card, which she inserted into the slot next to the door. A buzz signaled the door had unlocked and she walked into the lobby atrium that towered the height of the three-story building. The building was empty. No one would be in for a couple of more hours. Her office was on the second floor very close to the front of the building and looked out into the atrium below. Kate decided she needed the exercise after the 11 hour flight, so she ran up the open stairs to her office instead of taking the elevator.

Heading straight to her desk, she began to look over her mail and items in her inbox from the previous week. After about 30 minutes, she remembered she was here for another purpose. How easily I get pulled into work, she thought, and turned to her computer to look up any information relating to Buck. Just then, her cell phone rang, startling her so much it made her heart skip a beat. Gaining her composure, she saw that it was Jake.

"You scared me to death. I just sat down to the computer. Where are you?"

"I'm already at your house. I did find out my patient's name. It's Peter Meijer. I thought you might want to look up his name in addition to anything about Buck."

Kate asked about the spelling then found his name in the personnel file. Sure enough, there was reference of an interview in Texas, but no indication of any promotion or transfer pending. He was interviewing for the position of Lab Technician I, a position that requires very little training and skill and is usually recruited for locally. Why would they interview from Utrecht for such a low-level position? The expense of bringing someone over from The Netherlands did not line up with the salary paid a Lab Technician I. Something was going on and Kate knew she had to find what. She was responsible for all expenses at the Texas location and never would have allowed an extra expense like this. The more she sat thinking about these interviews and the cost involved, the more irritated she became.

Suddenly, she remembered the purpose of coming to the office was not to get caught up on work but to find out more about Buck. She refocused on her task and typed Buck's name on the computer to enter his personnel file. Nothing appeared to be out of line there. No indication he had missed any work. Everything looked normal, yet Buck was dead. He had died days ago, yet no one seemed to know.

Now was probably the best time to try out that back door into the lab's computer system. She reached into her pocket and pulled out the small piece of paper. She started to type in the address but remembered Buck's warning about getting in on the site and decided to enter from down in the training center. She could use a supervisor password that would allow her to access most areas on the business network. She didn't want to take any chances it could be traced back to her. As Kate left her office, she checked to make sure she was the only one on her floor. It appeared empty so she walked down the hallway, turned right at the next corridor and proceeded down the hall until she entered the training room. A dozen or so workstations faced one side of the room where an instructor's desk faced the training computers. A marker board hung behind the instructor's desk. Mounted on the ceiling in the center of the room was a video projector, used during training sessions. At a workstation in the far back of the room Kate revved up a computer. Within seconds it came to life with an entry prompt. Kate hesitated, took a deep breath, then typed: http://LansdunInternational/spprg/Tr/micro/4647and "enter." Just as Buck had directed, she typed in JCooper as the username and 8515 as the password. The screen changed to a blank blue background with a small spinning hourglass for a few seconds until it changed to the entry page of the lab site page.

Much to her surprise, Kate was able to access any page within the lab site. She smiled as she remembered Buck's genius with computers; he always knew how to make things work. After looking through the different pages she came upon a log page that seemed to be the lab director's notes, giving detail to all the activity in the lab. According to the log, something big was expected to happen this week. Another shipment was due in today, which would be the final component of the project they were working on. Only referred to as CF309, she could find no indication of what the project actually was. Kate checked her watch then continued to look for any mention of Buck or information involving the project.

Finally she gained access to the lab director's email file and went into the inbox. She scanned all email written and received since Buck first contacted her. Then she saw it. Beginning back in March, there were multiple emails concerning Buck McFadden. She flipped between the outbox and inbox and read that initially they were concerned about Buck's placement in the department because they were bringing in an outsider. Another email assured the lab director that he was the best man for the job. Then as she read each email, it became obvious they were concerned Buck was growing suspicious. In one email dated several weeks earlier, it was decided that Buck should come to Utrecht so he could be observed first hand by the directors of the project. There was one last email. It simply read, "Buck McFadden is no longer an issue. He will not be coming back to work in your department, situation has been resolved." Kate angrily thought, what a crummy way to communicate that you had just killed someone. "The situation has been resolved".

As she scrolled down the inbox a name caught her eye, her name, Kate Williams. Just as she began to open the email, she heard the door to the training room open.

"Kate, what are you doing here? I saw the light on and didn't realize anyone was even on the floor."

Kate caught her breath and turned to find Bill, one of the training managers that worked under her, standing by the door. "Oh, hi, I was just checking out a display setting on one of the computers in here. I was messing with mine in the office and got it out of whack, so I came in here to see what the setting was." She quickly exited out of the program, turned off the computer, and joined Bill at the door.

" I just got here. I came in early to look over a folder before the big meeting tomorrow."

"What big meeting? I've been out of town and haven't gotten to listen to my voicemail or check my email yet. In fact I'm not even supposed to be here until tomorrow. I couldn't sleep. You know, jet lag."

"It was announced Friday. You probably didn't get an email. I'm sure your secretary left you a voicemail. We're having visitors from Utrecht this week."

"Who? When?" Kate asked, thinking she already had an idea of the answer.

"Apparently, there are two members of the security team here to evaluate facility security and IS security. The meeting is at 11:30 tomorrow morning."

"I wonder why I haven't been contacted. I was just in Utrecht."

"It must have been a last minute thing. They'll be interviewing each member of the executive team. Some sort of security breach, I'm sure. Well, I need to get down to my office. See ya tomorrow."

Kate was flabbergasted. Not only had she not been informed of the meeting but this might be the last chance to get into the file and check the email with her name on it. She watched Bill walk down the hall and turn out of sight before going back to the computer in the corner of the room. Within seconds, she was back in the site and opened the email.

To: JJamison

From: FLiebmann

Johann,

Buck McFadden has been taken care of but we suspect he may have been communicating with Kate Williams there at the Texas facility. We have no proof of any communication between them but we do know that they have had a long friendship. She was in Utrecht last week. He was on his way to meet with someone but we failed to locate his contact. Whoever he was going to see would have known everything. We intercepted McFadden with a packet of information about the project.

Watch out for this Williams woman. I still suspect she is involved. Let us know if she is snooping around. If so, we will have to take care of it.

Franc

Great, Kate thought, what has Buck gotten me involved in? She printed a copy of the email at a printer in the training room, erased all traces of her accessing anything from the workstation and turned off the computer. She grabbed the piece of paper, folded and placed it in the front pocket of her slacks, and left the training room to go back to her office.

Kate's head was almost spinning, feeling the exact emotion she had felt the day she saw Buck killed. I need to show this to Jake, she thought, he'll know what to do. Once in her office, she turned off her laptop, placed it in its case, grabbed the rest of her stuff, and hurriedly left her office. She wanted to run to her car but instead regained her composure and walked out of the building.

She drove to her house and was relieved to see Jake's car in front. She pulled into her garage, got out of the car and hastily walked to the front door without closing the garage door. She opened the front door and was happily greeted by Jake. Without a word she turned and closed the door and snapped the lock shut.

"Hey Kate, I'm so glad you're back! You were gone longer than I thought you'd be." But as soon as he got the sentence out he saw from Kate's expression that something was wrong.

"You won't believe what I found. I am so freaked out. They suspect Buck was talking to me."

Who? Kate settle down. What are you talking about?"

"The people at the lab involved with the project, they think Buck was talking to me. They've alerted the lab director to watch out for me."

"Tell me from the beginning what you found."

"Okay, Jake, but I'm telling you we are in so much danger. I don't even know how I can go to work tomorrow. There's a big meeting with those guys we saw at Schiphol airport later tomorrow morning. Some sort of security investigation. I know they're here to watch me. What are we going to do?"

As they sat down on the couch Jake said, "Okay, start from the beginning."

Kate began by telling Jake she had located the files of the two men that were sent over for interviews from Holland. She explained that there was a record of their interviews but that the position that they interviewed for usually is filled locally and that their pay rate did not justify the expenses to get them here from Utrecht. She was very irritated with what she found because the expenses at the Triumph location were her responsibility and she had not approved the travel. She had to presume that someone higher up did the approval without her knowledge.

Next she related how she accessed the back door of the lab computer site on the intranet and that the username and password given to her by Buck must have been linked to the lab directors ID because it gave her access to everything including his email. She described how she scanned the sent and received email for information about Buck and saw that they had been suspicious of him since he arrived at the facility. Then she spoke about how shocked she had become when she read that he "has been taken care of". The last thing she shared was just as she found her name on an email, she had been interrupted by Bill, one of her coworkers. She described the meeting Bill said was scheduled for 9am tomorrow, and then about how she went back into the training center for one last look at the email. She pulled out the paper from her pocket and gave it to Jake.

"Okay, what am I looking at?"

"There in the body of the email, do you recognize a name?"

"Yours."

"Apparently they're suspicious of me. At least that's what the email says. Jake, this really freaks me out! We're in danger, just like Buck said. Why didn't I take him seriously?"

"Obviously we're treading into areas people don't want us to know about. But I still can't figure out what's going on. What we do know is that you received some emails from a friend at work. You saw him killed in Utrecht, but we have no body and no witnesses except the girl at the restaurant. We get home yesterday and find a package from Buck telling you to go snoop around and find out more information. Now we have an email that you found with your name in it. I agree that especially with those two thugs here in Triumph we are in danger, but we have nothing to tell anyone. Up to this point, with the exception of Buck's death, there is no evidence of any wrongdoing that we could communicate to any authority. I think the best thing to do is to lay low a while and observe."

"What do you mean, lay low? Stay here at the house?"

"No just go about business normally. Tomorrow you need to go to work and attend the meeting just as if you're not involved in this at all. The main thing is to be careful and to watch your back. And don't say anything about what we've seen or done. We don't know who we can trust."

"I don't know if I can just be normal."

"You have to. There's no other choice."

She leaned into Jake and kissed him, then kicked off her shoes and crawled onto the couch to snuggle up next to him. He reached over, put his arm around her, and pulled her close.

"I feel safe when I'm like this. I'm so glad we found each other."

"Me, too. I feel the same way when I'm with you."

They continued to hold each other as they looked out over the peaceful little lake. Storm clouds moved into view accompanied by the rumble of thunder in the distance.

"Looks like a storm's coming!" Jake injected into the silence. They both closed their eyes and drifted off to sleep as the lingering effects of jetlag took its toll on them. Little did either realize just how prophetic Jake's prediction of the storm would prove to be. Things were going to change very quickly.

After about five hours, they woke up to the end of a gentle rain. Jake went out to the screened porch. He could feel the mugginess of the air after an East Texas spring rain . He stared out over the lake and thought about all the events of the last two weeks. Despite the danger they might be in, he could not regret any of it since it brought Kate into his life. Being with her made him feel whole again. A feeling he had not felt for many years.

"What ya doing?" Kate asked as she joined him on the porch.

"Just thinking." He pulled her into his arms and kissed her. He then grabbed her by the hands and led her down the hall to the bedroom.

It was 5 pm before they both realized they hadn't had anything to eat all day. Kate got up from bed and headed to the kitchen. After looking through the fridge, she realized she had nothing at all she could fix. "We need to go to the store or go get something to eat somewhere. I am so hungry."

"I have an idea. Why don't we go to my house. I know I have something we can fix. Grab your things for work tomorrow and we can stay there tonight. It'll give me a chance to show you where I hang out when I'm not involved in international mysteries."

"That's a great idea. I was going to suggest we go to your house tonight anyway after finding out they're watching me I'll pack some things. It'll only take a minute."

As they were leaving, Jake remembered to grab the Beatles Album with Buck's information in it to look over again. Kate grabbed her laptop, briefcase, and overnight bag and headed towards her car. Within 5 minutes they were on the road to Jake's house.

Jake pulled into the garage and waived Kate's car in next to his.

"Just a little bit of house here," she said sarcastically. "This is incredible Jake. How did you ever find this place?"

"My parents built it. I spent a lot of my summers here. Wait until you see the inside and the view. I just love this house."

The house on the lake was originally his family's vacation home, built in the early 70's when Jake's family lived in Houston. It was a located on about three acres with 500 feet of lake frontage on the highest point that overlooked a cove on the eastern shore of the lake. His dad had been an avid angler and had built the house with relaxation in mind. A boathouse attached to a dock extended about 20 yards out into the water. At the end of the dock the decking extended into a large

30 foot squared area, half of which was covered and finished out with a built-in table for lakeside picnics. Jake spent many a summer day there swimming and enjoying the sun. Once they became teenagers, Jake and his sister Lauren, made use of the family boat to water-ski and fish with the large group of friends that frequented the lake each summer.

As they walked back up to the house, they passed a garden-lined path that terraced its way up to a large back patio lined with a stone wall just tall enough to sit on. A large screened porch reminiscent of the old sleeping porches sheltered the entrance into the back of the house. The front entrance to the split-level house led into a small gathering hall that stepped down into a tall A-framed great room with a fireplace centered on the back wall. On each side of the fireplace floor to ceiling windows provided a beautiful view of the lake. To the left a large open kitchen outfitted with commercial grade appliances to accommodate Jake's mother's passion for cooking over looked the main living area separated by a long breakfast bar. Placed around the bar were stools where the family could easily enjoy a casual summer meal. To the left of the kitchen a rustic dining area with a large wood-planked table perfect for family meals. On the right side of the living room a small paneled library that housed his Dad's book collection. In the corner sits the desk where Jake's dad used to make his fishing lures complete with the magnifying glass hung on a retractable arm. From the gathering hall at the entrance a staircase led up to a Master Bedroom suite on one side and two bedrooms and a shared bath on the other. All bedrooms looked through a wall of windows to a majestic view of Lake Triumph.

Although the house was over 30 years old, Jake is always amazed at how the design and character of the house still is way ahead of its time. Jake's Dad and Mom had done a superb job designing it. Simple rustic wood paneled rooms with hard wood floors everywhere except for the tile in the bathrooms. Jake's parents had always kept up with the care of the house. The same local family had been responsible for the landscaping, mowing, and housekeeping for the past 30 years. When

Jake moved into the house 10 years ago, he brought in a few of his things, yet for the most part the house remained very much the same as when his parents were alive. After Annette's death, Jake needed security and some stability, something he could hang on to from the past and the house was the only thing he had. Actually, Jake was living in the past, trying hard to forget about the deaths of Annette and his parents. Now for the first time in a very long time, Jake had a glimpse of a bright future with Kate Williams.

The garage door closed behind them as they walked through the utility room into the large kitchen. Jake, with Kate following close behind, moved into the living room set with large perfectly worn leather couches and chairs arranged around the big fireplace. Placed in the center was a large wood plank coffee table on top of a rug that covered only the necessary areas in front of each seat. Kate walked around and looked at every detail of the immense room, finally stopping in front of one of the large windows looking out onto the lake.

"This is absolutely gorgeous Jake. The views from here are breath taking."

"Since I moved here 10 years ago I made a pledge to myself that I would honor my parents by taking care of this great place."

"So, you live here alone?"

"Except for an occasional visit by Lauren's family, I'm here all by myself."

"Aside from the fantastic view, it must get lonely."

"At times. But there are many happy memories in this house." He smiled at her. "I hope the lonely days here are over."

Kate moved close for a hug. "I'll see what I can do."

Jake headed into the kitchen and wrapped a towel around his waist waiter-style. "What would be your pleasure Madame?" With a poor French accent, he added, "I can cook anything."

"So, I see you are a modest chef as well. Cook away, Chef Jake. Surprise me."

In a flurry of activity Jake began removing items from the freezer and refrigerator. After chopping, dicing, sautéing and browning, Jake presented a delectable stir-fry dish complete with a glass of white wine. He handed her the utensils and plates, then directed her to an outside table where they sat down to enjoy their dinner. A cool, fresh lake breeze topped off the evening.

With plates empty and stomachs full, they turned to the mystery that had obsessed them over the last week. The plan was simple: They would take it one day at a time and once they had enough information they would contact Chief Baker. As tomorrow promised to be a big day for Kate, Jake suggested they turn in as early as possible.

After clearing the dishes and cleaning up the kitchen, Jake grabbed Kate's bag and led her up the stairs to the master bedroom. A beautiful full moon beamed in through the windows, cascading a pool of soft light across the room. As they got ready for bed, Jake called, "Kate come here I want to show you something. Out here."

"What is it?"

Jake opened the balcony doors and moved out onto a porch with a small table and two chairs. "This is one of my favorite places of the house. I can imagine my parents probably spent some quality time out here."

They stood for a few moments, hand in hand, looking at the moon, both wondering what the events of tomorrow would bring. In the silence of the darkness they walked arm in arm back into the bedroom. They climbed into bed and held each other and gazed at the moonlight until sleep overtook them.

Kate woke up quickly the next morning as the sun shone fiercely through the window. She leaned over to Jake and kissed him on the forehead, waking him gently.

"I guess you don't need an alarm clock around here do you?"

He kissed her back and said, "Not with a beautiful woman bathed in the morning sun."

"It is rather bright in here. I guess you get used to it?"

"Took me a while, but now I hardly notice it."

It was 6:30 am and Kate was eager to get dressed and go to work and check her voicemail and prepare herself for the meeting to come. Since Jake was only working a half day they agreed to meet back at Jake's house as soon as Kate could get away from the office.

Kate jumped out of bed to shower. She got dressed, while Jake went downstairs to start coffee and breakfast. After about 30 minutes Kate appeared ready for work. Jake insisted that she have breakfast and coffee.

"Sorry, my plan was to bring you breakfast in bed, but you got up before me. Next time I'll set an alarm."

Kate looked up from her breakfast and replied, "Breakfast in bed? I'll take a rain check and hold you to it. That sounds great."

She finished her eggs and stood up to look for her laptop and briefcase, when Jake called out from kitchen. "Hey, your things are already in your car."

He walked her to the car, opened the garage, then opened Kate's car door. She stopped in front of him as he handed her his business card.

"You be careful, sweetie. Call me on my cell phone or at the office if you need me. If you call the office tell them I'm expecting your call."

Kate leaned over and kissed him and climbed into her car. She backed out slowly, waved and headed toward Lansdun. Jake looked at his watch and realized he had to act quickly if he was to make it to the practice on time.

Chapter 14
Sunday 1:30pm Amsterdam

Willem Voorhis boarded flight 47 to Houston from Amsterdam's Schiphol Airport on Sunday April 29 at 5:45 pm. He had never left the country without his family before; in fact he had never flown on an airplane alone before. This was a chance of a lifetime, the promise of a new job, and finally a chance to go to the United States. His dream was finally coming true.

The flight attendant directed him to 29B in coach class of a Boeing 777 that seated about 300 people. Willem was amazed that a plane with so many people on it could actually fly. Yet any trepidation or fear he had was replaced with the excitement of the plane ride. He studied everything around him, careful to catch every detail. As the plane doors closed and preparations were being made for takeoff, screens dropped down from the ceiling and a video started. An announcement directed passengers' attention to the image on the screen. In multiple languages including English and Dutch, Willem made every effort to focus on the instructions. He was very glad the instructions ran more than once.

The plane moved off the taxi way and onto the runway after waiting its turn to take off. As the roar of the engines vibrated the plane, a startled Willem grabbed the armrest and tried to calm himself. Within minutes the plane was airborne and climbed smoothly into the air until it reached cruising altitude.

During the first half of the trip, Willem enjoyed the meals, movies and even a nap or two. After about 5 hours the toothache hit again. He had hoped the pain was behind him. Ever since he had the work done by Dr. Metler, the tooth had hurt. It had never hurt him before, but he had trusted the advice of the seasoned Dr. Metler, and proceeded with the recommended root canal. Only now did he regret not checking with his own dentist before he had the procedure done. Willem hoped to ignore the pain, at least until he finished the interview process in Texas. Over the last week, he had been able to control the pain with ibuprofen. This new pain, however, was of an intensity he had not experienced before. Maybe it was because of the cabin pressure or the fact that he was sitting and not moving around. Whatever the reason, the pain was too intense to bear. He unbuckled his seatbelt, stood and opened the overhead storage bin to retrieve his small briefcase. He fumbled to get the clasp open and soon found his bottle of ibuprofen. Willem took 5 tablets even though he knew it was more than the recommended dose. He needed to get control of his toothache. He reached up and pushed the call button to summon the flight attendant.

"How can I help you sir?"

"A beer please! Heineken preferably."

"Certainly sir, I will be right back."

The flight attendant returned with the beer and handed it to Willem. Willem thanked her and took the 5 ibuprofen with his first swig of beer, then he downed the rest. Maybe the combination would erase the pain. He closed his eyes and drifted into a deep sleep.

After several hours, Willem was awakened by a gentle tap on the shoulder. "Excuse me sir," the flight attendant said. "Sir, please put up your tray table and raise your seat to its full upright position. We're landing soon."

Willem followed directions, relieved to find his tooth had calmed down. Please let it be okay until I get back home, he thought.

In Houston, he slogged through immigration and customs, relieved and excited that he had pulled it off with a fake passport. He had made it to Texas without tipping off his parents. After grabbing his luggage, he rode a bus to the rental car lot and minutes later he was in a nearly new silver mist compact that had been arranged by Lansdun International. A map made the 80 mile drive in the unfamiliar country easier that he expected. By 9:30 pm he pulled into the parking lot of the Triumph Inn. As soon as he entered his room, he dialed room service and ordered a small snack. Willem looked at his watch, still on Utrecht time, and thought it best to set his watch to Texas time. It had been a long day but with the 7 hour time difference between Texas and home, Willem was wide awake. He hoped he'd get some rest before the 1pm appointment at Lansdun the next day. The company car was scheduled to pick him up at 12:30pm.

He finally drifted off to sleep about 1am. Severe pain woke him from a deep sleep four hours later. The pain was much worse than it had been before. He hurried to the bathroom for more ibuprofen, then sat on the edge of the bed praying the medicine would work quickly. He was able to get some relief by sucking on ice from the ice bucket, but when the ice melted the pain returned just as bad as when it woke him up. He bent over and hugged his knees. "I have got to do something. This tooth can't get in the way of my interview. I need this job.."

After what seemed like an eternity, 7:30am arrived and Willem picked up the phone to call the front desk, hoping they could help him find a dentist that would take an emergency, then hung up. It'd be faster to ask in person. He dressed with the clothes from the day before and walked downstairs to the front lobby. He approached a young lady behind the desk. " Excuse me, I have a terrible toothache and I need to see a dentist right away. Can you help me?"

The young lady behind the counter looked up, initially disturbed that the quiet of the early morning had been broken. She listened intently, as if trying to decipher his Dutch accent, as he spoke again.

"I need a dentist, I am in terrible pain, can you help me?"

"I know just the man, my dentist, Dr. Jakob Patterson. He helps us out a lot here at the hotel. His office is right around the corner. Come with me to the front door. I can point it out to you."

"Dank u' well, I mean thank you."

"There right across the square. I know if you show up at 8 o'clock, he'll help you out. It's almost 8 now. If you hurry, they might be able to get you seen first."

Willem fast-walked across the square to the dentist's office. He reached for the door handle, just as someone inside unlocked it.

"Well, good morning," a young woman said, "My name's Kim. Can I help you?"

"I am so sorry about barging in but I have a terrible toothache and an important interview today. I need help please."

As she walked around to her desk, Willem hung his head over the open counter.

"Dr. Patterson will be glad to help you, sir. He'll be here in a few minutes. Here is some paperwork for you to fill out. We'll get you back to a room as soon as possible." She handed him a clipboard with a new patient questionnaire on it.

"Thank you, thank you," he said as he turned with the clipboard to find a seat.

Not long after he sat down, the office began to churn with business. Several patients walked in for their scheduled appointments. Kim greeted them by their first names with a friendly smile and offered them a seat.

Willem finished the paperwork and walked back to the window to give it to her, then returned to his seat, one hand holding his aching jaw.

Franny approached the back side of the front desk area and saw that a chart was already in the slot notifying her that a patient was ready.

"Franny, Mrs. Newton is here, but we have a toothache. Looks like a bad one. Why don't you go get Mrs. Newton seated and then seat the emergency patient and find out what he needs done. Dr. Patterson just called; he's on his way."

It was Monday and it looked to be a busy one especially since they were only going to be working the first half of the day. Franny was glad she had taken the time last week when Dr. Patterson was gone to get everything organized. Before she left last week on Thursday, she had set up for Mrs. Newton's procedure and in the other room she had set up for an emergency just as she did every day.

She grabbed a chart and walked to the reception room door and opened it.

"Mrs. Newton," she called, "Are you ready to come back?"

Mrs. Newton stood and moved toward Franny as she called out to Willem. "Sir, I will be right back for you in a minute."

Franny escorted Mrs. Newton to the first treatment room on the right side of the hall, then left the room to get the new patient's completed chart. The chart had a sticky note from Kim with his name spelled phonetically. Willem Voorhis. She opened the door and called hesitantly, "Willem? How do you pronounce your last name?"

Willem almost jumped from his seat. "It is Voorhees."

"I understand you have a toothache?"

"Yes, very bad, it has hurt for some time but it kept me up last night. I need some help, I have an important interview today at 1 o'clock."

"Come on this way." Franny led him down to the second treatment room. "Have a seat." She clipped on the patient napkin and asked, "Where does it hurt?"

"Right here." Willem said as he pointed to his upper right first molar.

"Let me take a few x-rays for Dr. Patterson." Franny took two digital x-rays. After the first one she saw it as soon as it popped up on the computer screen. There's that image again, the one on the other patient, she thought. She proceeded to take the next x-ray and asked when she was finished, "Mr. Voorhis, where are you from? Are you Dutch?"

"Yes, as a matter of fact, I am from Utrecht, do you know Utrecht?"

"No, but ever since Lansdun opened we occasionally will see a few Dutch patients. I am beginning to recognize the accent. But Dr. Patterson will be familiar with Utrecht," Franny replied. She was just about to tell the patient that Dr. Patterson was half Dutch when she heard the back door open. She excused herself and stepped out in the hall as Jake said, "Sorry I'm late, my first day back and all."

"Dr. Patterson," Franny whispered, "we have another one of those weird x-rays. It looks just like the one on the other patient, you know the one from Holland. Except this guy is really hurting."

Franny walked into the room first and pointed to the x-ray up on the computer screen. Sure enough, it was the same he had seen on the previous two Dutch patients and it was the same image as the logo next to Dr. Metler's name on his sign in Utrecht. Jake thought to himself, "Wait until Kate sees this!"

"Good Morning, Mr Voorhis, what seems to be the problem?" Jake chose not to share that he was part Dutch nor that he spoke Dutch. He did not want to drag out this appointment too long.

"I have severe pain Doctor. I need some relief. I have an important interview today."

Jake looked at the x-rays again and saw a large abscess around the end of the root. The tooth was severely infected and could not be saved.

"Mr. Voorhis, unfortunately the only quick help for you is to remove the tooth. You will feel much better with it gone."

"I need to be feeling better for my interview. If that is the only way, then take it out."

Due to the chronic infection around the tooth, the extraction was simple and without any complications. Jake renumbed the area with a long acting anesthetic that he hoped would give Mr. Voorhis relief through his interview. He wrote out several prescriptions and gave him directions to the pharmacy close to the Triumph hotel.

Before leaving the room, Jake slipped on another glove and reached over on the bracket table and picked up the extracted tooth. He gave a look at Franny that she immediately understood meant, "don't tell the patient I have his tooth." He carried the tooth back to the sterilization area and sprayed it with a disinfectant, then he wrapped it in a moist paper towel and placed it in a sealable plastic bag. He took it back to his office and hid the bag at the top of his bookshelf where no one could see it. He wanted to examine the tooth and call Kate, but he had patients to see. He wouldn't have a break until lunchtime.

Chapter 15
Monday Morning, Lansdun Facility
at Triumph, Texas

Kate arrived at work at 7:45. Foremost in her thoughts was the meeting at 11:30am. She wondered how she could she face the two men from Utrecht, especially since she knew one of them to be one of the guys involved in Buck's murder.

As usual her assistant was not at her desk. Annoyed, Kate walked past the empty desk and went about her morning routine. First thing was to check her voicemail. She had 35 messages. Kate took out a pad and paper and began to go through the messages one by one. She found one from her assistant late Friday afternoon informing her of the meeting . At least something was normal at Lansdun.

Kate had returned her phone calls and caught up on emails by 8:30. Now she had to make one more call. She needed more information about the meeting, so she dialed Greg Wilson, the facility manager.

"Good Morning, Mr. Wilson's office, how may I help you," answered Greg's assistant Paula.

"Hi Paula, this is Kate Williams. Is Greg in?"

"Oh Hi Ms. Williams, let me check for you." Paula put the phone on hold. "Ms. Williams hold for a second while I transfer you."

"Kate, welcome back," said Greg. "Glad you made it home safely. I assume you were notified about the meeting today."

"Yeah, I just checked my voicemail this morning. What's the meeting about?"

"We have two visitors from Utrecht. Seems that there have been some security breaches. I think these guys are here to go over protocol."

"That's funny. That kind of stuff usually comes through Operations. I would usually get wind of it first. Why all the fuss? Can't we take care of it locally?"

"That's about all I know. I only heard about these guys coming on Friday. I'm here in the conference room with them now. Come on down and meet them."

"Oh, I guess I can stop what I am doing. Sure I'll be right down. Bye." Kate caught her breath. *How can I face these guys? Be brave Kate, be brave.*

As she entered the conference room, Greg looked up and called out to her."Good Morning, Kate. Come over here. I want to introduce you to our guests." He turned to the men and said, "Gentlemen, this is our Director of Operations, Kate Williams."

Kate stepped forward and took the initiative to reach out to shake hands with the two men. "Good Morning, welcome to Texas!"

Kate recognized the man on the left as the one at the scene of the accident with Buck. He stood about 6'3" with short blond hair and blue eyes. He had a healthy pleasing smile and would have been considered handsome by most women, yet Kate saw a real toughness, having witnessed a brutal aspect of his character.

He reached forward and grabbed Kate's hand firmly."Hello I am Dieter Brach. Good to meet you! I understand you were recently in our country."

"Yes, I just got back from the annual meeting. In fact I'm still recovering from the trip."

"I understand. I too feel the time difference." He turned and introduced the man next to him, "This is Brit Vanheijsen, my colleague."

"Good Morning Mr. Vanheijsen."

Brit Vanheijsen took Kate's hand, shook it, but did not respond. It was obvious to Kate that Brach was the leader of the two. She couldn't wait to hear the content of the meeting to come.

"Gentlemen." She turned and addressed Greg. "Greg, I have a few things to finish before the meeting. I will be back at 11:30."

Kate walked out of the office, sweaty, heart racing and feeling nauseous and hurried to the restroom. She headed straight to the sink to wash her hands after touching the man that was involved in Buck's death. She moistened a paper towel, then placed the towel around her neck. The coolness began to calm her. Slowly, the sweatiness and nausea left and she began to feel normal again. Kate remained in the restroom for about 5 minutes before returning to her office. Her assistant, finally at her desk, seemed eager to find out about Kate's trip. Still thinking about her encounter with the men from Utrecht, Kate forced herself to act normal as she made small talk.

As soon as she could get away, Kate dove into her work, hoping to clear her mind of the encounter with the two thugs. The next couple of hours passed quickly as Kate worked to catch up from her absence the previous week. At about 11am Kate's assistant buzzed in and reminded her of the meeting at 11:30.

She grabbed a pen and her leather binder before leaving her office to return to the conference room. When she arrived, she took a seat in the back of the room. As she settled into her seat the rest of the executive staff filed in and took their seats for the meeting. Several of her coworkers turned and waived at Kate with a smile mouthing the words, "Welcome back!"

Greg Wilson stood up and asked for everyone's attention as he started the meeting. "As you know this meeting was called on Friday at the last minute. I appreciate everyone's cooperation in making time to attend. We have today two guests from the Lansdun headquarters in Utrecht. They are from the security team and are here today to talk about some important matters involving sensitive research conducted here at our Texas location. So, without further delay, I will turn it over to Mr. Dieter Brach." He turned to the side of the room and held out his hand to Dieter, directing him to the front of the room, then quickly stepped aside and moved to the back to sit next to Kate.

With a Dutch accent, Dieter Brach began to speak. "Good Morning! My colleague, Brit Vanheijsen, and I are here to speak to you today about a security breach that has occurred here at the Texas location. Recently it came to my department's attention that an employee here has compromised certain experiments. This man was in the IS department and was working in the high security lab located in the back of the facility. An investigation within our labs in Utrecht determined that certain sensitive materials were being smuggled out of the main lab. We are here today to inform you that Buck McFadden was this employee. Mr. McFadden was not here at the Texas plant for very long, so many of you may not have met him. Recently Mr. McFadden was called to Utrecht as part of this investigation where it was confirmed that he had a part in this deception. Unfortunately before this investigation came to an end, Mr. McFadden died in a traffic accident while shopping in Utrecht.

"We are here today to continue the investigation and to inform you that we will be interviewing many of you for information that may help us to find out more details. We will be contacting you throughout the week as we conduct our investigation. We appreciate your cooperation in this matter. Thank you."

Greg Wilson stood back up and thanked Mr. Brach, then concluded the meeting by asking for everyone's cooperation during the interviews. He pointed to the back table and told each member of the team to check the sheet for their interview time. Kate walked to the back and looked up and down the list for her name. Toward the bottom of the page she found her name and read, Kate Williams – Thursday 4pm.

Kate was speechless and numb. Switching back and forth from anger to panic, her mind raced. They're lying. They killed Buck. These guys were here snooping around. They're after me. Buck told me I was under suspicion.

Kate tried to call Jake and update him on the meeting but each time she called it went to his voicemail message. She wasn't going to leave a message. She needed to talk to him face to face.

The rest of the day proved to be routine but busy. Kate was always amazed at how much she fell behind whenever she was out of the office. But despite the busyness she felt that day, the words of Dieter Brach held foremost in her mind. What will I do when they want to interview me? I don't think I can do it. "Be strong Kate," she said silently, "Continue to be strong. You can do this."

Willem Voorhis spent the rest of the morning resting in his hotel room, lying flat on his bed at the Triumph Inn. Although he was sore from the extraction, the pressure and severe pain were gone. He began to question his desire for adventure. It was the first day of the trip and he had already had an emergency. Yet, he decided he had come this far so he might as well go to the interview. If things got worse, he could always go home. His parents would never need to know. Early in the afternoon, Willem left his room and took the elevator down to the hotel lobby. As he passed through the lobby to see if his ride to Lansdun was there he looked over at the counter and recognized the woman working behind the counter as the same person that had directed him to Dr. Patterson's office. He walked over to thank her.

"Well, well, you look so much better than I last saw you," said the young lady amazed that the young handsome man was the same one from this morning. "Did Dr. Patterson get you all fixed up?"

"He is an excellent dentist. Thank you so much for your help. Perhaps you have made it possible for me to get the job I am here to interview for today. Thank you again your help and generosity."

"I'm glad you're better, but no thanks is necessary."

"Good day, Miss." He turned and walked toward the front door and then exited to look for his ride. He sat down in front of the hotel and admired the view of the town square and hoped that one day he could call Triumph home.

The sound of a car pulling up in front of the hotel jarred Willem from his daydream. He blinked his eyes and saw a blue Suburban with the Lansdun logo on the door.

"Mr. Voorhis," A voice called out from the rolled down passenger window facing Willem. "Are you ready to go?" In an instant, the driver was out of the car and around to Willem's side, where he opened the door. The lanky man, dressed in pressed blue jeans, Lansdun golf shirt and cowboy hat directed him into the back seat. "Welcome to Texas," he said, loading Willem's bags into the back seat. The ride to Lansdun was about 10 minutes from town along roads lined with pine trees. Willem gawked at the dense forest of trees on each side of the road, certainly not what he expected to see in Texas. He had to admit he was a little disappointed that he wasn't looking at remnants of the old West or at least some cactus and or desert. At least he was riding with someone that sounded like a real cowboy. As they continued their short ride, the driver with a Texas accent told Willem of the history of the area and how excited everyone was when the Lansdun Plant opened. The openness and friendliness of the driver made him a little uncomfortable and ready for the trip to end.

"I was almost first in line when the job was first listed. Ever since then I've been driving this truck for Lansdun. So far it has been great. You here for a job, huh?"

As they drove toward Lansdun, Travis educated him on Texas, horses, rodeos and Houston. Time passed quickly and soon Travis called out, "Here we are. This is our turn. Over there on the right."

Willem noticed a small sign with the Lansdun logo at the edge of the driveway. The entrance road threaded into the forest for about a mile. The truck began slowing as it approached the entrance marked by the security building that monitored traffic entering and leaving the research center. The suburban pulled up to the window and the driver lowered the window to speak to the guard.

"Mornin' Brian. I have an interview candidate of Dr. Jamison in the High Security Area. A Mr. Willem Voorhis. Y'all should have paperwork on him."

"Got it." Brian waved them in.

The truck pulled through the gate and then passed the front entrance. The road continued around a large three story building to an area separated from the rest of the campus by another fence, then pulled up to a gate that opened when Travis punched a code into a keypad on a pole several feet from the gate. The trip ended in front of a doorway where a man in a white lab coat was waiting. As soon as the truck stopped, Travis stepped around and opened Willem's door.

"Hope your interview goes okay Willem, Good Luck!" Travis said as he shut the door and drove off.

"Mr. Voorhis," said the man in the white coat. "I am Dr. Johann Jamison. Welcome to Lansdun in Texas."

"Thank you sir, I am happy to be here." He noted that the Dutch man spoke to him in English. He wondered why he didn't greet him in Dutch, but his question was quickly answered.

"May I call you Willem?"

Willem nodded and the doctor continued, "You have no doubt recognized that we are kinsmen, but I feel it is important for us to speak English here so we don't make others feel uncomfortable. How is your English?"

"Very good, sir. I have been studying and using it for many years."

"Good, let us go inside, I can't wait to get to know you better." Dr. Jamison led the way into the high security area using his ID pass several times to open doors that led them deeper into the facility. He was, of course, more excited about the glass vial that Willem was carrying. He led them in through the lab which Willem noticed was empty. He had hoped to visit with his future co-workers to get an idea about his new prospective job. Dr. Jamison picked up on Willem's curiosity and spoke, "The lab staff is out at a meeting today in another part of the building. They will be returning to work later this afternoon to finish up their projects."

Dr. Jamison stopped at a door and opened it. He directed Willem into a large conference room and showed him to a pair of armchairs off to the side of the room. He pointed to the chair closest to the wall for Willem to sit in. Willem sat down and Dr. Jamison moved to a phone on the wall and spoke after pushing two buttons. "We are here now. You can bring it in."

Dr. Jamison moved to the other chair to sit when the door opened and a woman walked in with a tray holding two cups of coffee with cream and sugar and several cookies traditionally served with coffee in The Netherlands. Dr. Jamison nodded toward the woman and said, "Margaret, I'll take it from here." He took the tray and in a quick motion dropped a rapidly dissolving tablet of Rohypnol into Willem's coffee cup. Within seconds the tablet dissolved leaving no trace of the tasteless agent waiting to put the unsuspecting interviewee to sleep. Dr. Jamison hoped that the drug would work without any complications. He didn't need any problems like he had the first time he had used the drug, which had resulted in an overdose and the death of the interviewee. Although he was still able to retrieve the sample, the rest of the day proved to be challenging as he tried to figure out a way to dispose of the body. He smiled as he remembered how clever he was to put the body under the railroad bridge along with fishing tackle. He tried to make it look as if he had died while fishing. Fortunately, he managed to keep it from Franc Liebmann. He knew the project would be over if Franc ever knew he had killed one of the men sent from Utrecht.

Within minutes of Willem drinking the coffee, Dr. Jamison would ease the unconscious man back in his chair and remove the crown in his mouth, retrieve the sample then re-cement the crown. Each time he had done it before it was much easier than he expected it to be, yet he was more nervous this time. Perhaps because it was the last sample, the most important one, or perhaps because with this sample he had no more excuses for not perfecting the solar battery.

Johann set the tray down on the table between the two chairs and handed Willem his cup of coffee. He then sat with a cup in hand as he watched Willem doctor his coffee with cream and sugar. That was an activity Dr. Jamison always liked to see to ensure that any residual taste of the drug was masked by cream and sugar. It made the process so much quicker when the candidate drank the coffee quickly. This time was no different. Willem drank the cup as each had before, setting it back on the table after finishing the last drop.

Relieved, Johann sat back in his chair and began the wait for Willem to drift into a deep sleep. The drug usually took about 15 minutes to kick in, so Johann began the small talk as if this were an actual job interview. "How was your flight over?"

"Very well thank you," Willem responded. "It is my first time to Texas. I find it quite exciting. I have met many nice people. A helpful lady at the hotel and the driver that brought me here. It was a great flight except for the toothache I was having."

Johann continued to ask questions, not connecting Willem's toothache with the tooth that carried the last glass vial. "I am sorry to hear about that."

"It is okay now. I was in such pain last night when I arrived that I had no choice but to find a dentist this morning. Thank God I found a great man, Dr. Patterson. He saw me this morning and removed my painful tooth."

Johann turned white as the blood left his face, hoping that the tooth removed earlier in the morning was not the tooth he needed. He had to ask. He could not wait for Willem to fall asleep. "Where was the tooth?"

"Right here." Willem pointed to the upper right part of his mouth and the dark hole that graced the back part of his smile.

At that moment, Johann panicked as Willem confirmed his fears. He exploded in anger, "You idiot, do you know what you have done?" And without thinking he backhanded Willem across the face. Stunned, Willem fell backwards, ready to fight back, but the effects of the drug had begun to work. He fought the sleepiness, knowing it was time to end this adventure and go home, but he lost and slumped back into his chair.

Johann knew he had to work fast. He got up, slipped on latex gloves, and examined Willem's mouth. Sure enough the tooth was gone. What would he do? He only had an hour before Willem would fully awaken. Willem would forget that Johann examined his mouth, but he would remember being struck.

The last thing he wanted to do was call Franc Liebmann, but it was the only thing he could do. Time ticked away and he needed advice on where to go from here. First, the problem with Buck, then the guy with the overdose and now this. How could things have gotten so out of control, he wondered. As he punched the numbers on the phone to call Franc, he remembered the two members of the security detail that Franc had sent over to investigate the information leak that involved Buck McFadden. He put down the phone, rang the operator and asked her to page Dieter Brach. Dieter called back immediately.

"I need you in my office now! I have a problem." Jamison barked into the phone. Within minutes Johann was joined in the lab by both Dieter and his partner Brit Vanheijsen.

"What's this?" asked Dieter as he stood over Willem's crumpled form face down at the foot of his chair.

"The tooth is gone, along with the sample." Johann replied.

"What do you mean the tooth and sample are gone," Dieter asked with a stern tone.

"Today I was receiving the fourth and final sample from Franc Liebmann in The Netherlands. Willem Voorhis here, our courier, had the tooth pulled this morning at a dental office here in Triumph. I really didn't catch the name of the doctor.

Dieter reached down to turn Willem's face up and Johann realized how hard he had hit the unsuspecting man. The blow to the face had split his lip and opened a gash in his chin. In just a few minutes, Willem had bled all over his face, neck, shirt, and down onto the carpet. The bleeding had stopped but the wounds were still moist as they continued to clot. Bruising was beginning to show on the right side of his face.

"Oh, my goodness, I must have hit him really hard. I probably cut him with my ring." He said holding his hand up for the other men to see.

"Dr. Jamison, apparently you knocked him out with the blow to his face along with the rohypnol. This is not good. He will be one angry guy when he wakes up. Brit, put him in that chair over there and tie him up. We don't need him causing a problem when he wakes." He glared at Jamison. "Mr. Liebmann is not going to like this at all."

Chapter 16

Lunchtime came at the end of a short schedule. The staff left for lunch together and would return in an hour, so Jake had to work quickly. He decided to take more x-rays of the tooth that he had extracted earlier that day. He went back to his office to retrieve the tooth and returned to the sterilization area. After donning gloves, he removed the tooth from the bag and scrubbed it with an old toothbrush to make sure it was clean of any residual blood or debris. He then took it to one of the operatories to take five different x-rays. He verified that each shot had a clear digital image, then proceeded to take close-up digital photos of the tooth from the same directions he took the x-rays. After looking over the photos, Jake examined the inside of the crown. He held the tooth firmly in his left hand, then with a sickle scaler, he lifted the crown easily off. Much to his surprise when the crown came off, a small glass container popped out of the inside of the tooth. The inside of the tooth had been prepped and shaped exactly to fit the container hidden by the crown.

He picked up the small glass container with cotton pliers to examine it more closely and could see that the container held a cloudy liquid. Jake attached a stronger macro lens to his digital camera to look more closely. With the stronger lens he could barely make out what looked to be microorganisms of some sort. He needed more magnification, but didn't have access to a microscope.

He, instead, focused on the inside of the crown. As soon as he cleaned out any cement left in the crown, he saw the symbols clearly. Why didn't I think of that, he thought, it makes so much sense,. There on the inside of the crown was the white porcelain letters embedded in the metal. They looked exactly like the logo on the dentist's sign he had seen Utrecht: Dr. Jan Metler.

Jake turned his attention back to the small glass vial and tried to figure out what it could possibly be. How could he get a closer look at the liquid in the vial? It then dawned on him, Kim's mom. Kim's mom, Bonnie, was a medical technologist at the hospital. Maybe he could get her to help him out. Jake picked up his cell phone and called Kim.

"Kim, this is Dr. Patterson."

"What can I do for you, Doc?"

"I need a favor. Can you arrange for me to meet your Mom at the hospital this afternoon to look at a specimen under the microscope?"

"Well, I know she's at work. I can call her and then get back to you. Is everything okay, Dr. Patterson?"

"Kim, I called you because I know I can trust you."

"Of course you can Doc. You're okay, right?"

"Remember those funny crowns from the Dutch patients? You know, the ones with the symbols that show up only on the x-ray."

"Yeah, but why the microscope?"

"It's a very long story, but something's not right over at Lansdun. That's all I know right now. ."

"Okay, Doc. Let me call Mom. I'll call you back in a minute."

Jake hung up and dialed Kate. Her voicemail answered and he left a message, "Kate, I found something. Call me back."

As soon as he hung up, Kim's name came up on the screen.

"Okay, Doc. It's all set up. Mom said to come right now. Everyone's at lunch; you'll have free reign of the lab. Anything else I can do for you?"

"You've done great. I'll tell you the whole story when I know more."

Jake backed up the data files in order to get a copy of the x-ray files he wanted to show Kate. He pulled the DVD from his computer when the copy finished and placed it in a plastic sleeve in his laptop case. He powered down his laptop and loaded it in the case. He carefully placed the tooth and vial back in the plastic bag, which he put in his shirt pocket. With his laptop strapped over his shoulder, plastic bag in his shirt, he turned and grabbed his digital camera by the strap and left the office.

Triumph hospital was only a two mile drive from the town square. Jake parked his car in the visitor parking lot right in front of the building and walked through the front door and stopped right before the elevators. The lab was located on the second floor at the rear of the building so Jake entered the first elevator that opened. Upon reaching the second floor, Jake took a right and proceeded down the long corridor until he came to the Medical Technology Lab sign hanging over a doorway. He opened the door and saw Bonnie seated there waiting for him.

"Hi Bonnie, Thanks for helping me out."

"Technically, I'm not supposed to do this but since you're on staff, it should be okay."

"Thanks Bonnie. It's not a big deal. I have a specimen in a little vial and need something that will focus through the glass."

"I know just the scope." She led Jake across the lab and showed him where to sit.

"Would you mind staying around to look with me? Been a long time since I had to look at anything under a microscope."

"No problem."

Jake moved the lens up and down to focus. What he saw confirmed his suspicions The cloudy solution contained millions of microorganisms. Although he couldn't identify what types of cell they were, they all seemed to be working together, almost as if a small machine.

Jake slid back away from the scope. "Bonnie, take a look and tell me what you think."

She moved in and focused the scope to her eyes. She was amazed. Indeed there were millions of microorganisms, yet even with her 30 years of experience as a Medical Technologist, she was not able to identify what kind of cells they were, only that she knew they were not human but probably of some plant origin.

"Dr. Patterson, these cells are from a plant. I don't have any idea what type of plant but I can tell you they are definitely not human. I can't make out what's happening but there seems to be some sort of pattern they're following. I've never seen anything like this in my 30 years as a Med Tech." She rolled her chair back from the scope and turned to face him. "Where did you get this? What is it?"

"I can't go into it now." He placed a hand on her arm. "But I'm meeting someone and then we'll go to the police."

Jake retrieved the specimen and got up to leave. Bonnie stopped him, "There were some dead cells in the specimen. We need to help preserve whatever this is." She walked over to a nearby counter and came back with a small container, which she opened. "Put the vial in this tube of warm liquid, then wrap it with this insulated cloth. That'll keep it from getting too hot or too cold. I have no idea how long those cells will stay alive."

"Thanks Bonnie. Please don't tell anyone that I visited today. Hopefully one day soon I can tell you what this is all about."

Jake left the lab with the specimen tucked safely in his pocket and headed home. Just as he was turning into his neighborhood, Kate called.

"I got your message. What did you find?"

"Let's talk about it face to face. Where are you now?"

"Still at the office. I won't be able to get away until at least 3 o'clock. As soon as I get out of here, I'll come to your house. I have some things to tell you too. We need to decide what to do."

It was 5 o'clock by the time Kate arrived. Jake had started dinner and poured a glass of wine to give to Kate when she walked into the house. He wanted dinner to be ready soon so they could get talking immediately. Jake was anxious to find out what Kate had learned. He had already contacted his friend, Paul Baker, Triumph Chief of Police, asked him to come over at 8pm. Considering what he found out today about the specimen that fell out of the tooth, he knew it was time to go to the police. With a murder, a cover up, and now the vial in the tooth, he felt he had no choice but to contact someone.

Kate pulled into the garage that Jake had left open for her, parked her car next to Jake's. She got out of the car with briefcase and laptop in hand and walked to the door pushing the garage door closed, before walking into the house.

"Where have you been," he asked sarcastically. "I have been slaving over the stove all afternoon and you show up late for dinner."

Kate grinned. "Well, well, well, aren't you the pitiful one." She put her stuff down and moved in for a hug, holding him long and tight before releasing him with a kiss. "What do I smell? I'm so hungry. "

"My specialty, Chicken Mushroom Pasta. Grilled chicken sautéed in white wine with mushrooms served over an angel hair pasta."

"Yum. When do we eat?"

"About twenty minutes or so." Just then a buzzer sounded. "Looks like the bread is ready to come out of the oven. Why don't you put your feet up, relax."

"Let me change first, then I can relax. Be right back." After about 10 minutes, she reappeared dressed in blue jeans, tee shirt, and flip flops.

Jake watched her come down the stairs and thought how good she looked in his home.

"Just in time. Dinner's ready. Bread, wine, and a little pasta and fresh vegetables, my favorite meal."

Feeling pampered, Kate sat at the large plank table which Jake had already set for dinner. As she sipped her wine, Jake set a plate full of food down in front of her. She could get used to this type of attention. "This is so good, Jake. You can cook for me anytime."

"My pleasure dear! Bon appetite!"

They quietly savored the first few bites, then Kate set down her wine glass and said,

"Let me tell you about this morning's meeting. Something's going on around there but I still can't figure it out." She told him about the two security guys and the meeting in the conference room. "The presentation was from the two guys we saw at the KLM counter at Schiphol, Jake. Their names are Dieter Brach and Brit Vanheijsen, and they're nothing more than two thugs from the security team, masquerading as company officials here to conduct an investigation. They actually named Buck as the reason for their visit, accused him of smuggling stuff in and out of the lab. They must have found out that he had discovered what was going on."

"What exactly did they say?"

"They said Buck had been called to Utrecht for an investigation and his death occurred during a shopping trip. I think they know someone has communicated with him here. And based on the email we found, I'm sure they think it's me."

"It does appear that someone is trying to turn the blame toward Buck and away from themselves."

"They plan to interview us all and I'm scheduled for late Thursday. Jake, I am not sure I can sit in a room with those guys."

"Maybe it won't come to that. I called Paul Baker."

"The chief of police? Are you sure we want to do that? Share this with someone else?"

"Kate , I've known Paul for years and I really trust him. Besides he has the connections and experience to get this figured out. At least by talking with him, we can decide our next step."

"I guess at this point we are really getting in over our heads. We do need help. It sure seems to be getting more dangerous. Okay, your turn, what did you find out today?"

"Just a second, I have something to show you." Jake went into the kitchen, then came back with the insulated vial. He unwrapped it and laid it down in front of Kate.

"What is that?

"This is what they're smuggling in. Inside this glass vial is some sort of microorganism and they look to be working in some sort of pattern or sequence. Almost like a machine of some sort."

"How do you know this is what's smuggled in? Maybe this is what Buck planned to tell me about."

"Kate, do you remember me telling you about the teeth, the ones with the logo or symbol in the crown that only shows up on x-rays? Remember the dentist office in Utrecht? The logo on his sign. That is the symbol on the x-rays."

"But where does the vial fit in?"

"My guess is that dentist is placing the vials inside these crowned teeth. A guy came into the practice, first thing this morning. He had a horrible toothache and was here for an interview at Lansdun. He fit the profile of my other two patients: Dutch, males in their 20's, and all had a logo marked crown on an endodontically treated first permanent molar."

"What do you mean by endodontically treated tooth?"

"Sorry. I was talking like a dentist. Endodontically treated means that each tooth had a Root Canal. It's obvious to me now that the dentist in Utrecht had prepared the inside of the teeth specifically for these small glass vials. Once placed, the vials would be concealed by the crowns."

"How do you know what's in the vials?"

"A Medical Technologist at the hospital let me use one of the microscopes during lunch today. Neither one of us was able to identify the microorganisms we saw except that they were probably from a plant. We both agreed they appeared to be working in unison. She fixed up this container for me so that whatever is in there is kept alive. Once I saw this, I decided to call Paul and get him over here to discuss this mystery we're involved in. He should be here any minute."

"I'm a little uneasy about this, but if you really feel we can trust him, I'm okay with it."

"I can trust him with anything. In fact he could be very helpful with his connections."

Chapter 17

It took several hours to get hold of Franc Liebmann in Utrecht. Franc had been in a meeting all afternoon and was not taking calls of any kind. As soon as Franc left the meeting he saw the multiple messages left by Johann and called him back immediately.

"Johann, this is Franc. I noticed you called but I haven't checked my messages yet. What is going on? I thought we agreed you would not contact me by phone."

"There is a problem with the last shipment. It never arrived."

"What do you mean?"

"The courier had the tooth removed because of a toothache."

"Well, where is it? Find it and go get it. You do realize that our careers and possibly our lives are at stake here. I have given you over ten million Euros to get this thing completed. Don't just call me up and say you never got the shipment. Find it or else!"

Johann didn't need to ask what he meant. All that he had to do was look across the room at Dieter and Brit and he had a good idea what Franc meant . He didn't want to ever cross paths with those two.

"Yes sir, we will get it done. Dieter and Brit are here with me. We will get it solved."

"Let me speak to Dieter."

Johann handed the phone to Dieter. Franc was furious at the latest kink in receiving the final cell sample. The only option was to try to get the sample from the dentist's office.

"My plan is to break into the dental office and look for the extracted tooth, yet I have several questions needing answers like: Who was the dentist? Where is the tooth? Moreover, did the dentist find the cell sample?"

"Johann, how long will the cells be alive? How much time do we have?"

"The cells would be alive for about 48 to 72 more hours. I know I need to get them back soon. There is little time to waste."

"Dieter will know what to do. Hand it over to him," Franc said confidently.

Johann had no doubt about Dieter's ability, but that was no comfort to him at all. All he could do was send Dieter and Brit out to get the vial while he readied the lab.

"We will take Mr. Voorhis with us. We will take care of him." Dieter told him. Johann didn't want to know any more details.

Dieter and Brit left the high security area in one of the company cars. They placed Willem Voorhis in the back seat of the car with Brit attending to him. Still unconscious, Willem would cause them no problem as they passed through the security area. At the plant exit, Dieter slowed at the guards' building to sign out.

"Evening Sir!" said the security guard.

"Evening," said Dieter, "We are taking Mr. Voorhis back to his hotel. He leaves tomorrow. He is not feeling very well and needs his rest."

"Okay folks, have a good night!" The security guard waved them through the gate.

As soon as they cleared, Dieter pulled over at the next side road. Dieter got out of the car and opened the trunk as Brit picked up Willem and walked to the back of the car. Suddenly Willem began to waken and moan. Dieter placed a gag around Willem's mouth, then bound his hands with duct tape. He followed with a quick blow to the face to knock him out again. He would not bother them for a while. Brit then picked up Willem and placed him in the trunk. They could deal with him later, after they found the cell sample and got it to the lab. Before they closed the trunk, Dieter checked the contents of Willem's pockets. A Dutch passport, several 800mg Ibuprofen, 40 dollars in cash, and a key to room 301 at the Triumph Inn was all that he found.

They drove to the Triumph Inn where all three men were staying. Dieter parked then they hurried through the lobby and to room 301, where they searched for any information regarding the dentist who had removed the tooth. They had about given up on finding anything when a bright yellow paper on the floor caught Brit's eye. At the top was a name: Jakob Patterson, DDS. The receipt. Now they just had to find Dr. Patterson's office and retrieve the tooth and the cell vial implanted within it. Had they searched his luggage they would have found out just who the young man was in the trunk of their car. Inside the luggage was his original passport showing his real name: Willem Van Hollenvat, a name they would immediately have connected with the CEO of Lansdun International.

Chapter 18

Jake got up to answer the doorbell as Kate began to clear the table. In the kitchen she rinsed each plate, then wiped off the table. Jake opened the front door to the smiling face of Paul Baker. They shook hands and shared a friendly embrace.

"Evening Paul, thanks for coming over here tonight. We have something to share with you."

As Paul walked in the door he asked, "We? Who's we?"

"Oh yeah, new news." He directed Paul's attention toward the kitchen and Kate. "Paul, this is Kate Williams. I'm not sure y'all have ever met."

Paul stepped over to shake Kate's hand and said, "Paul Baker, good to meet you."

"Glad to meet you, too, Paul. Jake speaks highly of you."

"Oh really? Doesn't happen often."

"Can I interest you in a glass of wine or something else to drink?"

"Well I guess it all depends if I'm here on a social visit or an official visit. Jake, what is it, social or official?"

"Well, we really need to talk to you about some things that have happened over the last few weeks." Jake pointed Paul to the big leather chair on one side of the fireplace while he and Kate sat on the couch. "This may sound a little crazy but we're at a point where we're over our heads and need some help."

"Okay guys, I'm all ears. How can I help?"

Kate moved closer to Jake and took his hand. "You start, Jake."

"Okay here goes. Kate works for Lansdun as Vice President of Operations of the Texas facility here in Triumph. She's been in Texas for about 2 years, right?" He looked over to Kate and she nodded. "About a month ago she ran into an old friend at work that she had known from when she was working out of Lansdun's New Jersey location. This friend, Buck McFadden, was working in a high security part of the facility here in Triumph. When she saw him she was surprised that he didn't really acknowledge her."

Kate added, "He never even came over to talk to me. That was so unlike Buck. He was a good friend to me when I went through a tough divorce, always there to listen and so easy to talk to." Kate stopped and looked to Jake, "Go on Jake."

"Maybe this part is something you need to talk about."

Paul listened intently and jotted down an occasional note as Kate talked about the email exchange and the meeting in the restaurant one night that Buck was so nervous about. "Buck was convinced there was something improper going on in the lab. That was when he first started talking about smuggling. I tried to do some snooping, but it's a secret lab and the security's impenetrable."

"Smuggling?" Paul asked. "Why didn't you come to me sooner?" He looked over at Jake with a disapproving glance and asked, "How long have we been friends? You know you can tell me anything. Especially something as serious as smuggling."

"Calm down. This is all recent. We just got back from Europe day before yesterday. We didn't have anything to tell you until today. Let us finish the story."

Paul sat back. "Why don't you start with Europe? How does that fit in? After landing in Amsterdam, what happened?"

Jake jumped in. "Well, last week Kate and I met up on a flight to Amsterdam. I was headed to the International Dental Forum Meeting and to see my grandparents. Kate was on her way to a Lansdun corporate meeting. During the flight over we got to know each other and agreed to get together in Leiden after our meetings. Once in Amsterdam, I went to The Hague and Kate traveled to Utrecht."

Kate cut in, "My meetings in Utrecht were pretty routine. Several days of briefings and reports topped off by my presentation on the Texas facility here in Triumph on the last day."

Paul scribbled notes as Kate continued.

"The night before the last day of meetings on Wednesday, I received an email from Buck. He asked me to meet him at a café in old Utrecht because he had some important things to share with me about what was going on in the lab he was working in at Lansdun. His last instructions were for me to go to the café and wait at a certain table by the bar facing the front door. I thought it was strange that he told me not to even acknowledge him until he sat down next to me. So after my talk I went back to the hotel and packed most of my things together to prepare to leave the next day. I rescheduled a lunch and made my way to the café. I waited there until --" Kate stopped as she began to feel anxious and choked up about the memory of Buck's death.

Paul noticed a change in the tone of her voice and said, "Do you need a break?" as he reached out to give her comfort.

"No, I can go on." She replied as Jake held her close as if to share his strength.

"Take it slow, stop if you need to."

"I'm okay now." She clasped here hands in her lap. "I could see Buck running down the street toward the café. He looked...panicked and disheveled. He clutched his briefcase in both arms and kept glancing back as he ran. Suddenly, a black Mercedes came out of nowhere and plowed into Buck, launching him about 30 feet in the air. When he landed on his head I could tell he was dead. I just sat there stunned looking out the window. Before I could react, a matching car pulled up behind the first. Two men jumped out and picked up Buck's body and threw it in the trunk of the first car. The second parked as the other car sped off. Then those two men and a third that got out of the car began to look from shop to shop for, I suppose, whoever they suspected was there to meet Buck. I recognized the last man that got out of the car as someone from Lansdun's security team that I had just seen during one of the briefings I attended. As soon as I realized that those guys were looking for me, I got up and ran out the back door and found my way to the hotel. I quickly packed up the rest of my things and left."

When Kate paused, Jake said, "It was about 6 o'clock that night when Kate appeared in the lobby of my hotel as I came out of a meeting."

Paul interrupted and asked Kate, "Did you contact the police? Did you tell anyone what you saw?"

"No, who would I tell? There was no body, no evidence. I didn't know who to trust except for Jake. In my panic my only thought was that Jake would know what to do."

"Okay, so let me get this straight." He looked down at his notes. "You saw your friend murdered, the body taken away in the trunk of a car, then realized one of the men was connected with Lansdun."

Kate nodded

"Then you left Utrecht to find Jake in The Hague."

Kate nodded again and continued, "During the train ride across the country to The Hague, I thought back about the emails from Buck and the meeting I had with him in Triumph. He knew something was going on in the lab where he ran tech support. He alarmed me that I might be in danger and urged me to be very careful. At the time I didn't take his words seriously. On the train they came back to haunt me."

"I still don't understand why you didn't go to the police over there."

"At first I wondered that too," Jake interjected. "But you need to hear the whole story before you jump to conclusions."

"Okay, okay, go on, what else do you have?"

"The next couple of days Kate obsessed about Buck's death. I tried to keep her occupied as we sorted this mystery out, by showing her the sites in Holland, but she always fell back into that place where she dwelled on Buck. So I suggested we go back to the scene of the accident to help her get closure. All along we were trying to make sense of it all."

"Alright continue."

"So we went back to Utrecht and went to a café adjacent to the one Kate was waiting in. There at the café we met a waitress who verified Kate's story. She had even called the police, but they didn't find anything. They even questioned whether she was making it all up. The poor girl almost lost her job over it."

Kate jumped in, "It made me feel a little better when Jake knew for sure that someone else had seen it."

Jake patted her hand. "I always believed you saw something. I just didn't know exactly what until the girl finished the story for me." He turned back to Paul. "We were walking back to the train station when I saw a sign, a dental office sign. One I recognized."

Paul looked puzzled.

"You need more background on this part. Prior to leaving for the Netherlands, I saw a patient, a Dutch man, in his late 20's, with a porcelain crown in his mouth like the one we saw in the morgue. I left you a voicemail about it before I went on my trip. He had an important interview at Lansdun. The symbol I saw on my patient and the similar one in the morgue was the same as the logo on the sign at the dental office. A "J" superimposed over an "M", for Jan Metler, the dentist's name that I saw in Utrecht. I didn't know until today what it all meant."

"Okay, go on," Paul directed.

"This morning I had a second patient. He fit the same profile as the other one: Dutch, twenties, here for a job interview, and with the symbol showing up on an x-ray. Except today, the guy was in severe pain and asked me to pull the tooth. He was afraid the pain and infection would keep him from his interview. After he left my office, I took x-rays and photos of the tooth from all different angles. I was curious about how the symbol showed up just on an x-ray, so I removed the crown from the tooth. As I did that, this glass vial fell out of the tooth." Jake carefully handed over the insulated container. "It contains little more than a drop of liquid."

"What is that?" Paul peered at the small container.

"I wondered that too. So I took it over to the lab at the hospital and looked at it under a microscope. You know Kim at my office, don't you? Her mom, Bonnie is a lab tech over in Medical Technology. We couldn't identify what we saw exactly, except that there were microorganisms working in some sort of pattern, like a machine."

"What in the world is going on here? I need to get this to the crime lab in Houston so it can be analyzed properly. Then maybe we can figure out what is really going on."

"Paul, remember Kate said Buck thought something was being smuggled in. I think this is how they're doing it."

"Appears that something is important enough to kill for. Anything else?" Paul asked.

"Kate, tell him about your day and what you found out."

"Paul, they're in town! Two of the men from the accident are here in Triumph. They met with our executive staff today. But first let me give you Buck's packet." Kate hurried to the Beatles White record album she had brought over from her house, then spread the contents on the coffee table before them.

"This was left on my front door. It shows more details about what Buck found at Lansdun." She pulled out the page that referenced the backdoor entrance to the lab's computer site Buck had set up for her. "Yesterday I accessed the site and found emails to the lab director referencing Buck's death. Another in particular caught my attention. An email with my name in it. They listed me as someone they suspected had met or communicated with Buck." Kate paused for a second, then continued, "Which leads me to the meeting today. The two men were in town supposedly to conduct an investigation on a security breach. They informed us in the meeting today that Buck McFadden was the one responsible for the breach. They then announced that Buck was killed in a traffic accident, and that he had been smuggling things into the lab. I was so mad when I heard it, but I had to act as if things were normal. They're interviewing all staff members over the next few days. Mine is scheduled later this week."

Before Paul could respond, his cell phone rang. "Chief Baker, how can I help you. What?" He paused to listen to the person on the other end of the phone call. "I'm here with him now. We're leaving right away. Be there in a few minutes!" Paul stood up quickly. "Come on, we need to go, you're never going to believe this but, Jake, your office is on fire. That was Lieutenant Grey on the phone. He's there now."

Paul led the way out of the front door, followed closely by Kate. Jake stopped to lock the front door and then caught up to the two of them just as they got to Paul's car. The drive, although only 15 minutes, seemed to last forever. They were all silent as they traveled back toward town. Jake thought about the beginning days of his practice and how much it had become a part of his life over the last 10 years, keeping him from losing himself in grief over his wife's death and keeping him anchored in the community, his home.

Chapter 19
The Fire

As they neared the vicinity of the practice, smoke rose tall in the night air, and the reality of the fire set in for each of them. Paul parked his car as close to the office as possible without interfering with the fire department. Triumph's two main engines angled strategically in the street near the back side of the office where most of the smoke seemed to originate. In front of the office, Lake Triumph's Volunteer Fire Department's pumper assisted with the fire. As they got out of the car, Jake immediately started toward the fire before being held back by Paul.

"Jake, you and Kate wait here out of the way. I'll go and check with the fire chief and see what he knows. It looks like the fire is almost out. We'll know in a minute what the damage is."

Jake stepped back out of the way. Kate stood at his side waiting until they heard the news of the damage. As they waited next to Chief Baker's car, they were joined by Franny, Kim, and Janna.

"Dr. Patterson, we got here as soon as we heard. Do you know how it started?" Kim asked.

"We haven't heard anything yet. Chief Baker just left us to check on things." Jake turned toward Kim holding Kate's hand. "You remember Kate Williams don't you?"

Kim and the other two girls nodded, then the whole group turned collectively to watch the fire. A gentle breeze bathed the huddled group in mist. Each of them wondered what impact the fire would have on their lives.

Jake could see Paul Baker near the front door of the office conferring with his lieutenant and the fire chief. The area around the office had been blocked off by road barricades connected by the yellow tape one would see at a crime scene. A firefighter scurried out of the building and joined the two chiefs and the lieutenant. Occasionally they all looked back toward Jake and then continued with their discussion. Within minutes, an ambulance with sirens screaming arrived on-scene. Policeman pulled the barricades back to allow it to pass. As the ambulance entered the cordoned off area, Paul began to walk with his lieutenant towards Jake, Kate, and the three women.

As Paul got closer he called out, "Jake we need to talk; looks like the fire was no accident. Why don't you and Kate follow me across the square to the Starlight Café. We can sit and talk there." He tuned to the three women and said, "Ladies if you could go with Lieutenant Grey, he has some routine questions for each of you that hopefully will help us with how this fire started."

"Sure." They all responded in unison.

Jake hugged the women goodbye. "Girls, as soon as I know something I'll call Kim and she can pass on any information. Hopefully, I'll call tonight." With that Kim, Janna, and Franny turned and followed the Lieutenant.

Jake looked back toward the office as Chief Baker led them over to the cafe. He stopped to stare when he saw two paramedics emerge from the opening of the office with a stretcher carrying what appeared to be a man. It was then that Jake knew this somehow had to be connected to events they discussed earlier with Paul. He hurried to catch up with the group, holding his questions until they arrived at the café.

Paul led them to a table in the back, away from the busyness that occupied the front of the restaurant. As they passed the counter he called out to the woman behind the register. "Betty, we need to visit.

Could you manage to give us some privacy. Oh and could we get some coffee, please?"

"Sure Chief," Betty replied. "No problem." As they walked by she looked at Jake and whispered, "I'm sorry about your office." Jake nodded. Kate, speechless, followed at Jake's side. Memories of Buck and the whole incident in Utrecht came rushing back to her as they took a seat at the table. The same table she had met with Buck several weeks earlier.

Jake was the first to speak. "The ambulance. Was that a body they brought out?

"Was someone caught inside with the fire?" Kate's voice trembled.

"Yes, a man was found inside, bound and gagged, just barely alive," Paul replied. "It appears that whoever started the fire left the man inside to burn. Most of the damage was in the back of the office towards the lab and the sink area off to the side. The dental rooms were heavily damaged by smoke and water. The rest of the office just got heavy smoke damage. We found the body several feet from the more heavily damaged areas. Seems our Triumph Fire Department responded quicker than the arsonist thought they would. From initial reports, it appears that the young man we found in there was unconscious when he was put on the floor." Paul pulled out of his pocket a plastic bag with a passport in it. "The passport is Dutch, his name is Willem Voorhis, does that name sound familiar?"

"That's the patient I saw this morning. The guy that had the vial in his tooth. The vial I gave you. He was the one smuggling the stuff in. How did he end up back at my office?"

"In addition to being a fire scene, it's now a crime scene. So you can't get back in there until we complete our investigation. I hope that sometime tomorrow we can let you in to assess the damages. You probably need to call your insurance agent and let him know what's happened."

"Paul," Kate jumped in, "If this guy found in the office was left for dead by whomever started the fire, it means they're looking for the vial in his tooth. They already know Jake pulled the tooth and they probably suspect he has the glass vial. Shouldn't we expect more trouble?"

"I'm already one step ahead of you Kate. I have several officers over at both of your houses watching for anything suspicious. All I need from both of you are the keys to your houses so we can search them. You both need to plan on staying here in town. I don't think it would be safe to go back to either house tonight. We'll talk more tomorrow, when we know about Mr. Voorhis' condition. With his identity confirmed, that officially brings Lansdun into this situation. Looks like I have a long night ahead of me. I may have to contact both of you throughout the night if I have any more questions. Let's plan on meeting for breakfast tomorrow morning at the Starlight Café. We need to decide whether Kate goes to work or stays out of the way for awhile. Jake, I know you speak Dutch, so I may need you to go to the hospital to speak with Mr. Voorhis tomorrow."

"No problem. I'll help out any way I can. But you know that the only hotel in town is the Triumph Inn. With those two thugs from The Netherlands in town I don't think I want to stay there and take a chance of running into one of them. I'm sure they're involved in this somehow. Dr. Jamison, the lab director, probably is too. Where do you recommend we stay?"

"I think the Triumph Inn will be okay. I'll have two officers watching out for y'all the whole night. If you stay there, we'll take good care of you. I would feel much better if you stayed there versus somewhere else."

Jake got up from the table and walked to the counter to pay for their coffee. As he approached the counter he called out, "Betty I need the bill for the coffees."

She looked up and said, "Dr. Patterson, with everything that's happened tonight, the coffees are on me. I'm real sorry about your office. That's such a shame. Did I overhear that someone was found inside. It wasn't one of the girls was it?"

"No, it wasn't one of the girls. I just saw them a few minutes ago. Betty, Chief Baker has all the lowdown on everything. Why don't you go ask him?" Jake was relieved when she almost ran back to the table to gather the latest gossip to share in tomorrow morning's coffee group at the restaurant. Jake checked his watch and saw it was almost 11pm. It had been a very long day and he wondered what tomorrow would bring.

Jake held open the door for Kate as they walked out of the restaurant together, his arm around her shoulders. He knew if Betty saw them together, it would be all over town within hours, but he didn't care.

Chapter 20

Two others, hidden in the shadows, watched the fire from across the town square. Dieter Brach and Brit Vanheijsen were out of options. At about 8pm that evening, they had arrived at Dr. Patterson's office. They devised a plan that after searching the office and retrieving the tooth, they would stage a robbery and set the office on fire and leave Willem to be burned alive inside the building. A perfect plan, they reasoned, to retrieve the specimen and at the same time get rid of their captive, leaving no trace back to them. The office was dark as they easily broke into the back door. With flashlights in hand they walked through the office and searched the trash. All were empty. Dieter sent Brit outside to the dumpster to look through the office trash. Dieter searched the rest of the office and then attempted to make the break-in appear to be a routine burglary. As he moved toward the backdoor of the office his eye caught a red bag coming out of a container. "Ah, yes," Dieter thought, "A tooth wouldn't be in the trash; it would be in a biohazard container." He scurried through the office and picked up any biohazard containers he saw and carried them out to the car. Brit heard the noise and looked up from the trash dumpster.

"Get over here," Dieter hissed. "I have all the biohazard containers. The tooth is in one of these, not in the trash. We can check them after we get rid of our hostage. Go get the body and put him inside up near the front office."

Brit looked around, and satisfied no one was looking, opened the trunk. He reached down and easily picked up Willem and threw him over his shoulder. Dieter watched as he carried the young man through the back door of the office. Even though he had known Brit for more than fifteen years, he was always amazed at his size and strength. After placing the biohazard containers in the trunk, Dieter lifted out a container of kerosene and followed Brit into the office to set the fire.

Once satisfied at the placement of Willem bound and gagged, Dieter opened the kerosene and slung the liquid throughout the office and then kneeled down to strike a match. He dropped it into the liquid. The fire roared to life. They turned, hurried to the car and sped out of the parking lot without lights, easily disappearing into the darkness.

After driving for several miles outside of town, Dieter pulled over to the side of the road. He walked back to the trunk, put on latex gloves he had taken from the office, then began his search through the biohazard containers. He searched each container thoroughly but neither the tooth nor the crown was in any of them. Angered, he realized he had to go back to the office to search again. He hoped he could still get in the building.

As they drove back toward town, Dieter's anger and frustration were about to reach a boiling point. Fear caused the anger. Fear that he had failed to retrieve the sample. Fear about what Franc Liebmann's reaction would be. Dieter was jolted from his trance by the sound of sirens. The sound at first seemed far away but then they were right behind him on the road. Horns were honking and lights were blinking as the fire engine raced up behind Dieter's car. Dieter pulled over to the right shoulder and let the fire engine pass. He followed the same path as the engine, then realized he and the engine were going to the same place. This was not a good sign. He didn't expect this small Texas town to respond to the fire as quickly as it did.

Unable to go back to the office, he drove around to the opposite side of the courthouse and parked his car. He and Brit got out and walked closer so they could see the fire. Three engines and two police cars accompanied the dozen firefighters busy at work. It would only be a matter of time before Willem's body was found. Although the cell specimen was not found, Dieter and Brit knew their work was done here in the United States. They walked back to the car and made their way to their hotel out on Highway 59. Dieter and Brit retrieved their luggage from their rooms and loaded the car. Dieter walked to the lobby and paid the bill for each room in cash. He didn't need anyone tracing his credit card back to Utrecht. Within several hours, Dieter Brach and Brit Vanheijsen were on the first flight back to The Netherlands. Dieter was not looking forward to the conversation he would have with Franc Liebmann when he returned.

Chapter 21

Jake and Kate headed across the street and down the block until they arrived at the entrance to the Triumph Inn. Triumph Inn had been open since the boom days of the lumber industry. One of the few remaining landmarks that marked the prosperity of the area during the 20's and 30's, the Inn sat adjacent to the courthouse. For many years neglect and a county poor economy plagued the Inn, yet in 1986, the county rebounded back to life and once again the Inn was back in the limelight. It was purchased by a major hotel chain several years later and ever since had been routinely updated and modernized. Today Triumph could proudly boast of its first rate hotel to accommodate its many guests.

Jake and Kate entered the hotel lobby through the front door and made their way up to the desk. On the way over they discussed whether they needed to be in separate rooms or share one due to the gossip that Jake was sure would be generated by Betty over at the diner.

"Jake, we don't need to worry about what other people think, do we?" she asked hesitantly. "I don't want to have to worry about that every time we go out together in this town. Besides with all that has happened today I don't really want to be separated from you."

"Kate, I was just joking when I said we shouldn't share a room. I'm with you on this one. Our relationship is our business and if Betty wants to gossip about it all over town then that's her prerogative. So, let's consider this discussion behind us."

Kate smiled and grabbed Jake's arm and held tight. "I'm with you Doc."

With Kate by his side, Jake walked to the front desk to check in. He recognized the young lady behind the counter as one of his patients, Kari Washborn.

Kari spoke first. "Dr. Patterson, I am so sorry about your office. That is just horrible. Was there really someone found in the building? It wasn't one of your staff members was it?"

"No, Kari." Jake replied. "I just saw them a little while ago and everyone is okay. It appears that the fire was set and that the person found was connected. I won't know anymore until I talk to Chief Baker in the morning. But now I need a room for the night. I need to stay in town until this fire thing gets figured out."

"No, problem Doc," Kari replied. "I have just what you need! Credit or Cash?"

Jake slid his card across the counter and paid for the room. Kari responded by sliding the room key back across the counter and asked, "Anything else I can do for you?"

"No, that's all I need. Thank you very much Kari." As he turned to leave Kate elbowed him in the side and gave him a look as if to say "you forgot something." Jake quickly realized he had not introduced Kate to Kari. "Kari, this is Kate Williams; she lives here in Triumph. You might have seen her in town before. She works for Lansdun."

"Kate, it's nice to meet you. We sure do appreciate the business you send us. In fact, we had one of your people in here yesterday. I pulled a double shift today and started at about 6am. He came down asking for a dentist." She directed her attention to Jake. " In fact, I referred him over to your office. How's he doing? He was miserable, in a lot of pain. I sure hope he's feeling better. He didn't look very good."

"I am pretty sure he is not feeling any pain anymore. We got his problem taken care of. Thanks for the referral, Kari." Jake turned with Kate and began to walk toward the elevator, feeling as if he had lied to Kari.

"Oh and Dr. Patterson, I sent you two other patients earlier this evening. They asked about you and I told them where the office was. They must have been here at the hotel visiting someone," she said with a big smile on her face. "They were from Germany or something like that. Actually, they sort of sounded like the guy I sent to you this morning."

Kate felt the blood rush from her face as she heard Kari talk about the visitors. Jake took one look at Kate and knew he needed to ask more questions of Kari.

"Kari, what did they look like?"

"Well, they were both big guys, blond hair, cut short. Almost like they were in the military or something. They seemed to be real interested in finding your office."

"Are they still here at the hotel?" Kate asked.

"Oh no, they left several hours ago. I haven't seen anybody around the whole evening except for when you walked in. It's been pretty quiet."

Jake replied, "Kari, thanks for all your help tonight. If you see those men again, would you mind letting me know?"

"No problem Doc. Have a good night." She then looked down and continued working.

The elevator doors opened and Jake and Kate walked in and turned to face the lobby one last time for the evening. Jake pulled out his phone and called Chief Baker. The call immediately connected with his voice mail."Paul, this is Jake. We're in room 222 at the Triumph Inn. Hope those officers get here soon to watch our door. Oh, yeah, the two men Kate talked about from Lansdun were here earlier this evening, looking for my office. Thought you would want to know. Keep me posted on things. Thanks." Jake hung up the phone and looked at Kate. "I guess all we have to do is wait for Paul."

"Jake, please don't introduce me to everyone as Kate Williams from Lansdun. That just sounds so impersonal. Why don't you just introduce me as your friend, Kate?"

"Does sound kind of business like, doesn't it? I see your point."

Jake and Kate made it to their room, Before long exhaustion set in. They fell asleep in each other's arms, unsure of what tomorrow would reveal.

They were awakened by a phone call from Paul Baker. Disoriented and confused, Jake answered the phone. "Hello."

"Jake, this is Paul. Meet me over at the Starlight Café for breakfast. I had a busy night and I have some more information for you. How about 8am?"

"What time is it now?"

"About 7:15. Can you make it by then?"

"Not a problem. We'll be there."

"Okay, see you then."

Kate peeked up from the bed with one eye open as she lay with her head on her pillow. "Who was that? And why did they call so early? What time is it anyway?"

"It was Paul. He wants us over at the Starlight Café in 45 minutes. We need to get moving; it's 7:15."

Jake jumped out of bed and made his way to the shower. After about five minutes, he was joined by Kate.

"Move over Jake."

"Kate, what a surprise." He grinned.

"Don't get any ideas. You were in the shower too long. Save your ideas for tonight. We don't have that much time this morning."

"I'm sure Paul won't have a problem waiting."

"Sorry sweetie, not this time. Get out, I need to wash my hair if I'm to look decent for the Chief of Police. He is kind of cute you know."

"Okay, I can take a hint. Out I go." Jake climbed out of the shower but not before giving Kate a kiss.

They arrived at the Starlight Café precisely 45 minutes after Paul's phone call. As they entered, Betty greeted them with a smile and said, "Hi y'all. Long time no see."

"Morning Betty," Jake responded. "I don't know how you do it. You're here to open and you stay all day til it closes."

"Oh, Dr. Patterson, it just seems that way. I get to go home for a while in the middle of the day. Well, you know what it's like to own your own business, too. You just do what it takes to get the job done. Chief Baker is in the back, waiting for you."

As they headed to the back, Betty followed with a full coffee pot in hand. As soon as they entered the back room, the Chief stood . "Sorry, I had to wake you up so early, but we have a lot to do today. Let's sit down and order breakfast, then I can tell you what I found out."

Betty interrupted, "Does everyone want coffee?"

Jake answered, "Yes Ma'am, I sure need a cup. How about you Kate?"

"Yes, thank you."

The trio looked over the menus and then ordered. Betty left the room to turn in the order but quickly returned carrying a tray with three glasses of water. Paul was anxious to share what he had found out but decided to wait until the food arrived so they would not be disturbed while he told the story. He made small talk until the food order was placed in front of each one of them by one of the other waitresses in the café. Betty hovered close by with the fresh pot of coffee, eager to catch any bit of gossip she could glean from the conversation.

"Betty," Paul called to her, "We need to have our privacy."

"No problem, I won't let anyone in here to bother us, don't worry."

"Betty,", Paul responded slowing down her name and lowering his voice.

"Oh, Chief, you mean me. Oh, okay, wave if you need anything." Betty left the room her mouth turned down in disappointment that she wouldn't have first access to any gossip.

Paul Baker waited until she was clear of the room, then began. "Jake, I talked with the Fire Marshall this morning and he said your office is a total loss. The parts that weren't burned have been ruined by smoke and water damage. It appears it wasn't an accident. There's evidence of kerosene residue. Somebody was trying to burn the place down. My guess is to conceal a crime."

"Why did they have to burn it down?" Jake asked, frustrated as he thought of the mess in his office.

"We're not sure. We checked your office for any evidence, but it appears that whoever did this had broken into a building or two before. This one was a real professional job. We did find something we know came from your office, though. Out on the side of Hwy 3105 just north of town, one of my officers found several containers with red bags in them. Nothing but a bunch of needles, bloody gauze, and teeth were found inside. There was one label from a packing slip in one of the containers that had your name on it."

"Why would someone steal your trash, Jake?" Kate asked.

"That trash is Biohazard waste. We're required to keep it separate from the normal trash in the office. Anything with blood, or body part like a tooth, as well as something like needles, have to be put into special trash. We have a service that picks it up once a month." Jake answered, still stressed about the whole fire.

"You put teeth in there?" Kate asked.

"Yes!" Jake responded as if hit by lightning. "Now I know for sure that whoever was in the office was looking for the tooth I pulled out. The one with the cell specimen inside. So I guess it is connected to all this mess."

"What about the man found in the office? Was it really the Dutch guy Jake saw yesterday morning?" Kate jumped in.

"We got positive ID this morning. We fingerprinted the man we found and checked with Lansdun International. "That and the interview with our patient confirmed his identity as Willem Voorhis."

"So have you figured out who burned down my office?"

"Our best hunch at this point is that someone was looking for something in your office and chose to get rid of Mr. Voorhis in the process."

"That means Willem was put in my office by someone looking for the vial containing the cells. So what's next?"

"Jake, I'm sure you have some details to attend to with your insurance company. So I suggest for the rest of the morning you touch base with your staff, insurance man, or anyone else that needs notification of the fire. I need you in my office at the police station at one o'clock. We're meeting with the FBI."

"The FBI? Why the FBI?" Jake asked.

"With the attempted murder of a Dutch national, I had no choice but to contact them. I called an old friend down at the Houston office and he'll be meeting with us. It appears they've been doing some investigation about this case already. We'll all find out more at one o'clock. And Jake, could you come to the hospital to talk with Mr. Voorhis? I figured since you already know him you might be able to get more of the story."

They finished their breakfast and left the restaurant, agreeing to meet at Paul's office at one o'clock. Jake and Kate were driven by a police officer to Kate's house so she could pick up some clothing.

While there, Jake visited with the officer assigned to watch the house, who told him there had been no visitors during the night. Kate returned to the patrol car and they proceeded on to Jake's house on the opposite side of the lake. Upon their arrival, the officer watching that house met them at the car and requested they call Chief Baker. Jake grabbed Kate's things and walked inside the house with Kate at his side.

"Wow, it sure feels good to be back home. Seems like we've been gone forever, even though it's been only one night." Jake picked up the phone, then sat on the couch. Kate stayed in the kitchen and began to make a pot of coffee..

"Chief Baker, how can I help you?"

"Paul, you wanted me to call?"

"I just wanted to let you know I'm pulling the officers from y'all's houses. I need them to work in other areas of the county. I'll still send a patrol officer by every hour to check. I'll be by in a few minutes so we can go over to the hospital to see Mr. Voorhis." Paul paused and said, "I need to speak to Kate too."

"Sure thing." Jake handed Kate the phone.

"This is Kate."

"Kate, how would you feel about going to work this morning? I think things need to be normal around there. We don't want to arouse anymore suspicion about you. We might need your contacts in the future. We'll be keeping an eye on Lansdun from a distance. "

"I never really thought that I wouldn't go in today until you mentioned the meeting at one o'clock. I was just going to take the day off, but since you mention it I better show my face there today. Who knows, maybe I can find out some more information for your investigation. Anything else?"

"No, that was all of it. So I guess I'll see you at one o'clock. My office right?

"Right, see you then."

Kate put down the phone and looked over at Jake. "I guess I am going to the office for awhile. Paul thinks it best if I show up this morning. I need to head up stairs to change." Kate climbed the flight of stairs to the master bedroom.

"Be careful Kate," Jake whispered as she disappeared into the bedroom.

Chapter 22

Kate drove to the Lansdun facility and arrived at the security gate at about 10:00 o'clock. She showed her ID badge to the guard on duty and easily passed through security, then moved to the parking lot where she pulled into the parking space with her name on it. Within minutes she was in through the front entrance and up the stairs to the hallway outside her office. As she walked into her outer office she saw her assistant busy at work.

"Good Morning Sue," Kate called as she walked into the room.

Sue looked up and replied, "Good morning. Kate."

"Any news or calls for me this morning?"

"Greg Wilson called about 15 minutes ago looking for you. He asked me to have you call him when you get in."

Kate was somewhat relieved that Greg was the only call she had and that there wasn't any news for her. She sat behind her desk, put her laptop in the docking station and turned it on. After a few minutes she was able to sign in to the network and access her email. The only unread email was one from Greg Wilson. It very simply stated. "Kate: call me as soon as you can."

Kate picked up the receiver and called him.

"Greg Wilson's office, how can I help you?"

"Paula, Kate Williams here, I'm returning Greg's call. Is he in?"

"One second. I know he's expecting your call."

Moments later, Greg was on the line. "Kate, it's about time. I sure have news for you."

"What is it?"

"You know those guys that came in from Utrecht and gave the presentation yesterday? They're gone. They left this morning to head back to Utrecht. Something about being needed at headquarters for something. Can you believe it? After all the hassles they put us through yesterday rearranging everyone's schedule to set up meetings with them. One minute we're supposed to give them access to everything and the next minute they're gone. Something crazy must be going on at corporate headquarters. Was everything okay when you went over there last week?"

Kate knew better than to try and interrupt and respond to Greg's questions. She knew from past experience that Greg sometimes would get like this. He didn't want a response. He just needed to vent. "Uh-huh." She mumbled in response.

"It appears that some interviewee from Utrecht was here yesterday. Did you know anything about this? Since when do we interview men from The Netherlands for jobs we can recruit for here in Texas?"

"I was not aware that anyone from The Netherlands was coming over to interview. For what job position?" As she spoke, she thought of the poor man in the hospital that was found in the fire.

"This guy was apparently interviewing for a position in the high security lab. I discovered that several others have interviewed over the last few months, but none have been hired. Brian over at security alerted Paula this morning. He just thought it was a little strange that the one from yesterday that arrived at about one o'clock in the afternoon left later not feeling well. He said he left with those two guys who gave the briefing. Something is going on and I am going to get to the bottom of it."

"What do you propose we do?" she probed, realizing this information tied the two men to the fire and the body found there.

"I'm already on it. We're scheduled to meet with Dr. Jamison over at the high security lab in about 15 minutes. I need you there. Maybe we can get some answers with both of us. I'll swing by your office in about 5 minutes and we can head over there."

"Are you sure you need me?" Kate responded hesitantly.

"I can't do it without you. You have to be there. You should have been told what was going on."

"Okay" she replied, knowing there was no way out of it. "I'll be ready when you come by."

Kate felt extremely uncomfortable about this turn of events. How would she be able to face Dr. Jamison? Was he directly involved in Buck's death and the attempted murder of Willem Voorhis, the man found at the fire? Panic began to creep in. As she recalled all the scary things that had happened over the past week, she realized she was caught up in a deadly mystery. She took a deep breath, regained control and picked up the phone to call Jake to tell him where she was going.

Jake recognized Kate's number and answered his cell on the first ring. "Kate, what's up?"

"I made it to work and found out a few things that Chief Baker might find interesting. Did he pick you up yet to go to the hospital?"

"No, I'm still waiting. He just called and said he was delayed a little bit. Should be here anytime though. How long have you been there?"

Answering his own question Jake continued, "Thirty minutes and you already have new information?"

"As soon as I got here my assistant told me that Greg Wilson wanted me to call him. You remember me telling you about Greg. He's the facility manager here, basically in charge of all the research projects. Anyway, I called him and he began ranting and raving about the two guys that were here yesterday. He told me that they had gone back to Utrecht in a hurry. He was so upset that they came in yesterday and disrupted everyone only to disappear today."

"That's a little strange for those guys to leave so quickly, you don't suppose that--"

"Don't get ahead of me now. He went on to say he just heard there was a guy from The Netherlands interviewing for a job here yesterday. I assumed he approved the interviews but apparently he knew nothing about them. He said he also found about the other interviews. Oh, yeah, I almost forgot, one of the guys with security informed him they saw the guy leave early yesterday evening with those two men. He thought that it was a little weird so he called Greg's office to let him know. Maybe this is the link Chief Baker needs to connect those two to the fire."

"Wow, your day has sure moved along quickly. I know Paul will find all of that very interesting. So I guess then I will see you at one o'clock. "

"One more thing. Greg wants me to go with him to talk to Dr. Jamison in the high security lab. He's insistent on getting to the bottom of these interviews from the Netherlands. I'm kind of freaked out about going over there, especially since I read those emails with my name mentioned."

"With Greg there I am sure it'll be okay. Just listen and find out as much information as you can."

"Thanks Jake. I just wanted you to know what was going on over here. What about your morning?"

"Well, I talked to my staff. We're meeting so they can divide the list of patients and inform them of the fire, if they haven't already heard. I have a call in to my insurance agent. Hopefully, he can get over and assess the damage so we can decide what our next move is. For the time being I am out of business."

"I guess I'll see you at one."

"Be careful and listen well. Call me when you're leaving and maybe we can get some lunch before going to visit Paul."

Kate hung up the phone and waited for Greg to come by her office. She had wanted to get access to the lab for a long time. Now that she was finally able to get in there she wasn't looking forward to it at all.

Moments later Greg stuck his head in the door and asked, "You ready Kate?"

"Sure." She stood and followed Greg who was already on his way down the hall towards the high security area. The whole time they walked, Greg complained and repeated the conversation they had had earlier in the morning. He was not happy at all. Perhaps it was good she was with him to help tone down their conversation with Dr. Jamison.

The Texas Lansdun Facility was shaped like a big U and had 3 floors all looking out into the pine trees that surround the property. Parking was all around the periphery of the building. The center of the U had three separate buildings particular to the kind of research that each one housed. One of the buildings, about 10,000 square feet, was the home of the high security lab overseen by Dr. Johann Jamison. As they walked toward the back of the building, both of them occasionally stopped and said hi or checked on their teams. Kate thought how good for everyone to see her and Greg working together as a management team. So many times the research side of the house and the support side seldom worked directly together, which over time had created a small division in the workplace.

Dr. Jamison waited at the door of the facility as Kate and Greg entered. He shook their hands, greeted them with a smile, and spoke in Dutch-accented English, "Good morning. Why don't we visit in our conference room where we can have some privacy. Would you like some coffee? I can have some brought in."

Greg responded, "No thank you. Kate, you?"

"No thank you, Dr. Jamison. I'm fine."

"So, why do I have the pleasure of your visit today?" Jamison asked.

Greg answered after briefly looking at Kate and getting a nod. "Dr. Jamison, it has come to our attention that you have interviewed several men from the Netherlands. I'm concerned that prior to now neither one of us was aware that interviewees were coming in from overseas." Greg paused then continued, "I guess we have some questions as to why we are considering these men for employment and who is covering the cost of their travel to and from Utrecht." He then looked over to Kate indicating she needed to continue.

"Dr. Jamison, it is just unprecedented to spend so much money to bring individuals in for an interview, especially for a technician position. In the past we have always recruited locally for this position." Kate spoke keeping her cool knowing what really was going on with the men.

As Greg and Kate spoke, Dr. Jamison's face turned red as if he was going to explode. When he spoke he blurted out, "I can not believe you are questioning who and how I interview. My lab has been authorized to function as I need it to for my research. If you have any questions about it then you need to talk to Franc Liebmann in Utrecht."

Kate made sure to look him in the eye when she said, "I understand how you feel Dr. Jamison, but the travel, hotel, and expenses are showing up in my budget. So it does impact my world. I am not telling you who to interview, but I do need to know ahead of time so I can prepare for how it will affect our budget."

"You come down here and interrupt my important research just to ask stupid questions. I will be contacting Dr. Liebmann about this intrusion." His back rigid, he added, "This meeting is over. I am done now. Please leave my lab."

Greg was angry and Kate had seen that look before so she quickly intervened and took over the conversation. "Well then, I guess our visit is over. Greg let's go back to your office and figure out how we can write this up in our weekly report." She turned to Dr. Jamison and said, "Thank you for your time, you will be hearing from us again and I am sure you will be hearing from Franc Liebmann."

They both turned to walk to the lab exit. Dr. Jamison walked behind them without another word and looking somewhat uncomfortable. He followed them to the door and watched just long enough to see the door close. He turned and walked back to his office where he grabbed his cell phone and hastily dialed Franc Liebmann.

Greg and Kate walked in silence back to their office building. Halfway down the hall Greg broke the silence, "Kate, thanks for taking charge there. I was sure to lose it if we had stayed any longer. Dr. Jamison was out of control and he was getting me there too. Don't you think it a little odd that he reacted so explosively, so quickly? I can think of a hundred ways to react over that scenario short of a temper tantrum. I wonder what that guy is hiding?"

"Maybe we'll all be surprised when we get to the bottom of this. Let me know what happens when you get a hold of Franc Liebmann."

"Don't worry, I will. We need some answers."

"Greg, I have an errand to run this afternoon, but I'll have my cell with me. Call me if you learn anything new." Kate turned and walked down the hall to her office. It was only then that she realized how empowered she had felt while in the meeting with Dr. Jamison, knowing all that he had been up to.

Meanwhile, Paul Baker picked up Jake and they traveled the short distance to the hospital at the edge of town. On the drive over, Jake filled Paul in on the new developments at Lansdun that Kate had shared with him .

Chapter 23

At the hospital, Jake and Paul made their way to the 3rd floor intensive care unit to check on Willem Voorhis.

"How is our patient this morning, Carol?" Paul asked as he approached the nurses' station.

"Chief, he is finally coming out of it. When he arrived he was heavily sedated so we haven't had a chance to talk with him yet. Looks like the gag he had around his nose and mouth probably saved him from a lot of smoke inhalation, but we've supported his breathing with oxygen throughout the night. Whoever put him there had him knocked out pretty good. Whatever it was kept him sleeping all night long. Other than the contusions and cuts on his face, I think he'll come out of this just fine. Certainly a close call! Another 30 minutes or so in the fire and he would have been toast. Makes me appreciate our Triumph fire department." Carol looked over at Jake and remarked, "Dr. Patterson, I'm sorry about your office. I hear it was a total loss. At least Mr. Voorhis wasn't killed in the fire."

"Thanks Carol. I appreciate your sentiments. The whole town has been very supportive."

Chief Baker interrupted, "Carol, can we see our patient now?"

"Oh sure Chief, he is in room 310a just down the hall. Your officer is sitting in front of the door. Go on in. Maybe he's awake now."

Paul and Jake went down the hall, entered the room and stood at the foot of the bed looking at Willem Voorhis. Almost as quick as the door closed, Willem began to stir and his eyes opened.

Still somewhat groggy he looked over at Jake and spoke to him in English. "Dr. Patterson, where am I, did I pass out? This is not your office" His bloodshot eyes scanned the hospital room. Then his head fell back down on his pillow, eyes closed. "Wait, I remember now. I left your office, went back to my room and rested until the interview. I made it to Lansdun and then the rest is all a blur. What happened? Why am I here in the hospital?"

Jake responded in Dutch, "Willem, you are hurt but you are a lucky guy. We found you bound, gagged and unconscious in my office that had been set on fire."

"You know Dutch?" Willem queried.

"Yes Willem, I never got a chance to mention when we first met that my mother was Dutch and I spent most of my summers visiting my Oma and Opa in Leiden. They have turned their home into a hotel, Hotel Leiden, perhaps you know it?"

"Yes, in fact my parents stayed there when they came to visit me once last year. This world we live in certainly is a small place."

Before Jake could ask Willem what he meant about his parents visiting him in Leiden, Paul interrupted, "What is he saying? Translate for me."

"I'm sorry Paul." Jake turned back to Willem and asked, "Willem, can we continue in English? This is Chief Paul Baker with the Triumph Police Department. He really needs to hear what we're saying. Is that okay with you?"

"Of course, that would be no problem at all. I am quite comfortable with English."

"Oh good" Jake replied. "Willem, I examined your tooth that I removed yesterday. Were you aware that you had a glass vial inside of your tooth?"

"What do you mean? I don't understand."

"It appears you were being used to smuggle a glass vial containing a cell sample into the country intended for Dr. Jamison at Lansdun."

"I did not know that. I wondered why I needed the crown and root canal, but I wanted the job badly, so I could move to the United States. I wanted to visit my family dentist for a second opinion, but at the last minute went with Dr. Metler's recommendation. I should not have ignored my gut feeling. What a mistake I made."

"Son, you were put into a dangerous situation. It almost killed you back at that fire," Paul said. "You had no idea you were carrying anything in your tooth?"

"No sir, I thought I was just interviewing for a job. They had no idea who I am."

"What do you mean? Of course they did. You're employed at Lansdun, interviewing for a transfer."

"Oh, I have made such a mistake. I should have stayed in Leiden. I could be going to school now. I just wanted to get away."

Jake moved around to the side of the bed and rested a hand on the railing. "Willem, what are you talking about? Is there something else you need to tell us?"

Willem hung his head and took a deep breath. "My real name is not Willem Voorhis. My name is Willem Van Hollenvat. My father is Rijkaard Van Hollenvat, CEO of Lansdun International."

Surprised, Jake asked, "What in the world are you doing here in Triumph, Texas applying for a lab-tech job?"

"I just wanted to get away from my life. Do something completely on my own without my family having any influence. My parents are going to be really upset with me. I should have just stayed in school in Leiden. I'm working on my degree in Biochemistry. Right now my boring, predictable life back home doesn't seem so bad anymore."

Jake thought the young man was close to tears. Chief Baker filled in the gaps for Willem on what probably happened once he got to the interview at Lansdun. He followed up with a few questions, then left to go back to the police station. Jake stayed behind with Willem. With Chief Baker gone, the conversation returned to Dutch.

"Dr. Patterson, thank you for everything you have done for me. Having someone here that is familiar with my home makes things a little easier. I am still not sure how I am going to tell my parents."

"Don't worry Willem. Once they know you are alive and well, I am sure they will greet you with open arms. You probably will have a lot of explaining to do, but things will be all right. We are all grateful you are okay."

"Yeah, I am very nervous, but yet really thrilled to be going back home."

"I overheard the nurses saying that you should be able to get out of the hospital tonight. If you need a place to stay until you leave for home, I have plenty of room at my place."

"Thank you Dr. Patterson, I didn't know what else to do.

To change the subject and put the young man at ease, Jake asked, "So you know my Oma and Opa?"

"I just met them once when I came to meet my parents at the hotel. Your Oma was very kind."

They talked about Leiden, the university, Willem's classes and the little apartment that Willem shares with his roommate, until Jake realized it was time to leave for the one o'clock meeting with Paul. Jake promised he would be back at the hospital later to pick up Willem and take him out to his house on the lake.

On her way back towards town, Kate called Jake to let him know she was leaving her meeting at Lansdun. It was about quarter to one when she got to the main road to town and they decided that it was best to meet at the police station. As she pulled into the parking lot of the Triumph police station, she found Jake, leaning back against the front of his car, arms and legs crossed looking as he didn't have a care in the world. Little could anyone tell what they both had been through during the last two weeks.

On their way inside Jake got Kate up to speed on the recent information he had learned about Willem during the morning. And at 1 o'clock sharp when they walked into Chief Baker's outer office, Paul's secretary was waiting on them and led them down the hall to a conference room to meet with the Chief and a representative from the FBI. Both men stood as they entered the room. The Chief directed Jake and Kate to seats across the table from where they were sitting.

Still standing, Paul introduced his colleague. "Jake, Kate, this is Grady Hoffman, the agent I was talking about."

Agent Hoffman smiled, stood up and reached over the table to shake both of their hands. Mid 40's, dressed in a dark suit, he looked the stereotypical FBI agent.

"Agent Hoffman and I have worked together many times in my former life down in Houston, isn't that right Grady?"

"To put it mildly." Hoffman chuckled. He then looked over to Jake and Kate, "Triumph, Texas, has one fine police officer here. I hated to see him leave Houston. He was a big help to me many times."

"Thanks, Grady. I'm very glad you got here to help us with this mess that seems to have just sprung up here in Triumph overnight." Paul directed his attention back to Jake and Kate. "Agent Hoffman and I have spent the morning going over the details of the case. I think I have him briefed on everything I know but I'm sure he has some questions for you. Agent Hoffman, I guess I'll turn it over to you now."

"Let me begin by saying it appears you two have been through a lot over the last week and a half. Why don't we just start from the beginning? First, I want to you to know that an agent that is head of our Sub office in The Hague is on his way, as well as a representative from the Dutch National Police. We should be able to meet with them later the evening. As soon as Paul contacted me last night I contacted him about our meeting today. He wanted me to wait until he arrived but Chief Baker had already set it up with you two. At least I'll be able to get the investigation going on this end before they arrive. He should be here at about 6pm. I believe he may have an interesting proposition for both of you."

Jake interrupted, "Agent Hoffman, Paul must have told you about Willem Van Hollenvat. Having the head of Lansdun's son involved must complicate things further."

"It is much bigger than you think and you guys might have just helped us to break this thing wide open. A little history about our investigation: About two years ago the US Department of Defense and the Dutch Ministry of Defense began a coordinated research project located in Utrecht in the Netherlands. The project was biotechnical and centered around developing a better solar battery for the next generation military uniform. Both countries recruited their best scientists and little by the little the project began to make progress. Unfortunately, that's all I can share about the project since it's high security."

Agent Hoffman shifted in his chair, then continued, "About 9 months ago a scientist that had previously worked for Lansdun left the project to return to his old job." He looked over at Kate and said, "I believe you know him, Dr. Johann Jamison."

"Yes, in fact I just met with him and the facility manager, Greg Wilson, this morning. Greg wanted to discuss with him the Dutch nationals he was bringing in for interviews. Dr. Jamison got very defensive when we questioned him about these men and stopped the meeting after only a few minutes, then escorted us out of the lab area."

"Well, as you and Jake have already shared with Chief Baker, Dr. Jamison was smuggling critical components needed to complete his research from the Netherlands in the teeth of these men. We knew that it was arriving here somehow but I have to admit that smuggling cell samples in the molars of teeth is a first for me. Pretty ingenious though. Without the information you found we may have never figured out how they did it. Apparently he was close to a break through, and needed these components to help construct the final part of his research. We know a lot of money exchanged hands with certain individuals over at the Utrecht Solarcel project. There are still a lot of pieces left to be discovered which is why we were excited to find out that you had some information coming from a different angle."

Over the next several hours, Agent Hoffman asked exhaustive questions over and over again until he was able to repeat the story back to them. Around 4 o'clock he looked at his watch and said, "We don't have much time. They'll be landing soon."

"Landing? It will take him about an hour and a half to get up here from the airport," Paul stated.

"Oh, didn't I mention that they were flying a private charter to the Triumph airport?"

Jake sat up in his chair. "I almost forgot about Willem. He's supposed to get out of the hospital this evening and I invited him over to my house."

"Don't worry about Willem," Paul reassured Jake. "He'll be meeting the plane with us. I've sent an officer to pick him up and take him to the airport."

Agent Hoffman slapped a hand down on the table. "We have just enough time to get something to eat. Know any good places around here?"

"Sure do." Jake smiled. "Guess we're headed back to the Starlight Café. Wonder what today's special is?"

After a late lunch or early dinner at the café, Paul drove Jake, Kate, and Agent Hoffman out to the airport. The Triumph airport was located out of town about five miles to the east, a typical airport found in many mid size towns in Texas. Two runways crossed in the middle with a hanger located off to the side. Routine traffic for the airport was three or four planes a day, mostly single engine planes. Hardly enough traffic to keep a small airport in tip-top shape but since the arrival of Lansdun to the community, contributions from the company kept the airport in good shape for the occasional shipment that might arrive or depart from the Texas plant. Only occasionally would a jet land in Triumph and word traveled fast in Triumph. In a few days everyone would be aware that the FBI and the Dutch National Police were in town.

As soon as they pulled into the parking lot, the Gulfstream G450 slowly dropped out of the sky to make a perfect landing on the East/West placed runway. The jet taxied over to the edge of the tarmac approximately 100 feet from the hangar. When the engines wound down to a stop, the door near the front of the jet opened and a stairway folded out. Several men in black suits walked down and positioned themselves on each side of the stairway. Agent Hoffman walked with Paul, Jake and Kate over to the plane. He flashed his ID and then climbed up the stairs, followed by the rest of the party. Once on board they were escorted to a small conference area toward the back of the plane. On one side of the narrow aisle was a couch for two people. The other side had two captain's chairs facing a small table attached to the side of the plane. The chairs rotated toward the aisle, designed for a small meeting. Agent Hoffman directed Kate and Jake to sit on the couch and Paul was pointed to a seat further back in the cabin. Rising from one of the captain's chairs to greet his guests was Agent Michael Porter, bureau chief of The Hague sub office. He introduced a distinguished looking man in his mid 50's as Peter Hart ,the representative from the Koninklijke Marechaussee, or royal marshals, known as the KMar.

The group sat down as Agent Porter spoke. "I want to start the meeting by thanking everyone for everything that you've done so far. Let's start by reviewing what you discussed with Agent Hoffman today and then we have a proposition to discuss with you." For the next hour Agent Hoffman led the briefing with Jake, Kate and Paul filling in gaps.

Then Agent Hoffman looked up from his notes and began. "It appears the investigation has moved pretty far along. The events of the last week filled in a lot of the gaps for me but also brought in some other situations that make these crimes even more profound." He stopped and looked specifically at Jake and Kate, paused, then continued, "Now that you know that Willem Voorhis is really Willem Van Hollenvat, son of Rijkaard Van Hollenvat. Mr. Hart is here to help with the investigation. Willem has been missing for several days. His disappearance has gotten a lot of attention back in The Netherlands."

Mr. Hart spoke, "Rijkaard Van Hollenvat has asked me personally to make sure Willem gets home safely. We will be conducting a thorough investigation to determine how he ended up here and what events led to his near death. Mr. Van Hollenvat is very grateful for all you have done so far. Agent Porter is working closely with my office to see that there is a quick resolution to this investigation." He looked to Agent Porter.

Agent Porter added, "You two have experienced a lot over the last two weeks. Without the help of each of you, our case would be stuck where it has been for the last six months. Thank you for all the sacrifices you have made."

Kate looked and smiled over at Jake. "I can't think of anyone I'd rather be in danger with. Not exactly a recommended way to start a relationship."

Jake smiled back "I have to admit it has been a crazy two weeks."

"Now it is time for us to take control of the investigation. We appreciate everything you have done for us. Kate, with your connections at Lansdun and, Jake, with your ability to speak fluent Dutch and the knowledge you already have of the case, we need to ask you both to help us out. Hopefully, with what I am about to ask you to do, we can solve this smuggling and corporate espionage case and arrest those involved in Buck McFadden's death."

"Agent Porter," Paul jumped in, "I don't think it's fair to ask them to continue to risk their lives anymore."

"Hold on there, Chief Baker," Agent Porter responded. "What I am proposing is that they help us close this mess. They will be watched and working with our agents as well as those of the Dutch Royal Marshalls at all times. Besides, they're already involved. Of course there will be danger involved but they will be safer than they have been the last couple of weeks."

Jake interrupted the two men, "Excuse me. Paul, let us make the decision once we hear what he's going to ask. Whether we like it or not, we are involved. I think we can decide whether or not we want to continue to be involved."

Kate nodded. "Well said Jake. Agent Porter what do you want us to do?"

"We know that Dieter Brach and Brit Vanheijsen went back to Utrecht without finding the cells that were smuggled in by Willem Voorhis. My plan is that Kate and Jake contact Franc Liebmann and let him know you have the cell specimen and will be willing to sell it back to them for a handsome sum. Let's say three million Euros."

"Do you think they'll take the bait?" Jake asked.

"Considering what they have spent already to get the components from Solarcel, 3,000,000 Euros is a small price."

"Okay, I'm in. How about you Kate?"

"Count me in, too."

Paul interrupted, "Wait a minute guys, you don't even know the plan. Hear him out please."

"Thanks Paul, okay where was I? Oh yeah. We will have you meet the contacts in Utrecht. At some café somewhere, possibly an open air café."

"I know just the place. Kate, it's that outdoor café in old Utrecht. Right adjacent to where Buck was run down. It's perfect."

"We'll need to check it out first. According to you, that's close to Dr.Metler's office too, isn't it? Sounds like it could be an ideal location for the meeting. We need to act on this quickly. My suggestion is that we leave for The Netherlands as soon as possible. I'll get the plane ready for departure as soon as it gets refueled and the flight check is done. Our pilot, Curtis, said he can have the plane ready to go again in an hour if necessary. How soon can you two be ready?"

"What about work? If I don't show up tomorrow it could look suspicious," Kate asked.

"I'll leave that to Chief Baker and Agent Hoffman to take care of. They'll continue the investigation here in Triumph. Paul, do you think you can visit with..." Porter stopped and asked Kate, "Greg Wilson right?" He then continued, "Paul can you visit with Greg Wilson and tell him Kate will be gone for a few days?"

"No problem, Agent Porter," Paul replied.

"We don't need to make Dr. Jamison suspicious. We'll wait to contact Liebmann until Kate is out of the country. I'm sure it won't be long before he gets word of Kate and Jake trying to sell back the cells."

"Okay," Jake replied, "Agent Porter, I need a couple of things if we are to do this for you."

"What's that?" asked Porter.

"A ride back home and a few days of relaxation in the Netherlands for Kate and me. There are some sights I didn't get to show Kate last time we were over there. Our trip got a little interrupted." Jake responded with a smile.

Kate added, "Agent Porter, I just need to run home and get a few things. I can be ready to go in an hour."

"Jake, you okay with an hour?"

"No problem."

Paul drove them back to their houses to get packed while Agent Hoffman stayed behind and made sure Porter had everything he needed to continue the investigation. The plan was that Chief Baker and Agent Hoffman were to continue the investigation in Triumph but only after they knew that Kate and Jake had landed safely in The Netherlands. Paul would contact Greg Wilson and inform him that Kate would be absent for a few days on official business. During the drive Paul made sure his friends were comfortable with the decision they were making and that they knew all the risks.

Within an hour, both of them had packed their bags. When they arrived back at the airport the plane was fueled and ready. They said their goodbyes to Paul, thanked Agent Hoffman and climbed up the stairway into the plane, ready to embark upon the rest of their adventure.

Chapter 24

As the plane took off, Jake took a few minutes to introduce Kate to Willem Van Hollenvat, who was already seated on the plane when the couple boarded for the trip across the Atlantic. After a few minutes of conversation with Willem, Kate and Jake moved back to the conference area to meet with Agent Porter, who briefed them about what would happen during the next 24 hours. With the time difference, they would be arriving in The Netherlands mid-morning the next day. After landing at Schiphol Airport, they would drive to the FBI office that Agent Porter ran in The Hague and meet with the FBI and representatives of the Royal Marshalls involved in the case. Afterwards, they were to send an email to Franc Liebmann to inform him of their desire to meet with him to sell back the smuggled cells. In addition to the cells, they would sweeten the deal by including the information that Buck McFadden had sent to her from Utrecht before his death. They would spend the night in The Hague and leave for Utrecht as soon as a meeting place was established. FBI agents would go to Utrecht ahead of Kate and Jake to check out the meeting place and determine how to keep it secure.

With the briefing over, Kate and Jake began to feel the effects of a very long day. Although the cabin was a lot smaller than the commercial flights, the seats were much more comfortable. Neither of them had any trouble falling into a deep sleep.

Jake awoke as the warmth of the mid-day sun heated up the window he leaned against as he slept. Although he woke disoriented and confused, he soon remembered how he ended up on the airplane. He checked his watch, amazed to see he had slept for about 9 hours. Jake straightened up his chair and looked over to Kate, still sleeping soundly. It was hard to believe that it was less than two weeks ago when he and Kate began their relationship on their first trip to The

Netherlands. What a whirlwind it had been since they started seeing each other. He was so glad to have Kate in his life.

Within a few minutes, the captain's voice came over the plane's PA system. "Morning folks! Sorry to wake you, but we are starting our final descent and I need to prepare you for the landing. Go ahead and get your seats up-righted and we will be landing soon."

Kate began to stir and one eye opened, looking towards Jake. "Is it morning already? I must have really been tired."

"The captain just let us know we're on final approach. We should be on the ground in a few minutes."

"Good. I need to stretch my legs and walk around. I must not have moved much at all," Kate said with a yawn.

"I was out too. I only woke up a few minutes before you."

Seconds later they heard the bump and rumble of the landing gear as it dropped out of the plane to prepare to land. Jake leaned to look out the window as Kate looked over his shoulder. There below them was the Dutch countryside, flat crop lands interspersed with small square patches of flowers and dairy pastures, each field lined with a narrow irrigation channel. The sky was over cast and a hint of rain waited for them when they landed. All and all it looked like a typical Dutch day.

The plane landed and proceeded to an area isolated from the rest of the airport. As it pulled up to an unlabeled hanger, several cars approached the plane. Two men got out of each car to wait for the door to open. Inside, the main cabin steward opened the door of the plane and let the stairs down to the tarmac. As Jake looked out of the window he saw four men climb the stairs. The first two to enter the plane were Dutch Immigration and Customs Officials. They very quickly approached each passenger and asked to validate their passport. As quickly as they arrived, the officials turned and left the plane, returned to their car, and drove away from the plane.

Agent Porter remarked as the other two men boarded the plane, "Looks like we're cleared with Immigration and Customs."

Jake replied, "Sure is a lot easier this way than coming in on a commercial flight. That was very efficient."

"Yeah, it's definitely nice when they come out to us. Each time it seems to be less of an ordeal." Just then the other two men came aboard and sat down next him. "Jake, Kate, this is Bill Henry and Jason Loving, they're from my office in the Hague. They'll take us to my office so we can meet with representatives from the KMar." Both men shook hands with Kate and Jake.

Before leaving the plane, Jake and Kate said goodbye to Willem and Mr. Hart. "Willem, now I'm going to hold you to your promise. I expect that tour of Leiden when we get there in a few days," said Kate.

"Of course Kate, I'm looking forward to it. You have all my contact numbers, right?"

"I have them. I'll call you as soon as we arrive at my grandparents' house," Jake responded before Kate could answer.

Jake shook Willem's hand and Kate gave him a hug before they exited the plane.

The trip to The Hague by car was about 40 minutes via the main roads running south from the airport. As they drove into town, traffic increased and the slow-down on the Utrechtsebaan added another 20 minutes inching through town until they arrived at the FBI Sub office located in the American Embassy. They pulled up to the gates of the Embassy and the car was waived on through.

Jake and Kate were both in awe as they walked into the Embassy. Although located in another country, the entry to the building gave them a feeling of home. Winding stairs on each side of the foyer surrounded the entry hall. The FBI sub office was located on the second floor and Agent Porter led the small group up the winding stairs, then down to the end of a long hall. There on a door facing them was the familiar seal of the FBI. Once inside, they headed to a conference room to await the rest of the party.

Within minutes two men representing the KMar joined them. Agent Porter introduced them as Jeroen Debeer and Thijs Roeleveld. The two described how they were involved in the investigation of the disappearance of Willem Van Hollenvat. The KMar had been informed by Willem's parents that he had been missing for several days. Recently they became aware of Willem's trip to Texas and were making plans to travel to Triumph on behalf of his father to convince Willem to return home, but then learned of his situation. Their mission now was to work with the FBI to close the file on this case. They thanked Kate and Jake and pledged the support of Lansdun's resources and the KMar.

Because the attempted murder had occurred on US soil, the KMar agreed to take a secondary role in the investigation yielding to Agent Porter and the FBI. Agent Porter showed Kate and Jake the email that would be sent to Franc Liebmann at his Lansdun email address.

FLiebmann

Mr. Liebmann,

We have obtained the cell sample that you are missing. It is still alive and stable. We demand a payment of 3 million Euros. Once the money is received we will turn over the sample and information obtained from Buck McFadden prior to his murder. You must respond to this email by 1800 hours or the cells and information will be turned over to the proper authorities.

You will be told of a meeting place with wiring instructions for the money once you respond.

Kate Williams

KWilliams

Chapter 25

Franc Liebmann had almost lost all hope of rescuing the project until he opened his laptop after lunch and saw the email from Kate which provided a much needed glimmer of hope. He had just spent the morning with Dieter Brach and Brit VanHeijsen after they returned back to Utrecht. With the project now in a shambles with seemingly no way out, Dr. Jamison missing the last component needed to finish the project and two men killed in the process, the future of the project and his career looked very dim. However, Kate's email presented the possibility that all these problems could disappear. She demanded three million Euros, a small price to pay to get the last part of the cell mix and any information that might implicate him in the Buck McFadden murder. Yet the information she had to share troubled him. She was a loose end that would need to be taken care of. One more death would have to take place. Dieter Brach would know what to do.

The meeting with Kate would still need to take place. Franc had to know what information she had concerning Buck's murder and of course he needed to get the cell sample back. The email back to Kate was simple.

KWilliams

I am intrigued by your email and am interested in meeting with you. Please let me know the time and place. No police.

Franc Liebmann

FLiebmann

Franc Liebmann's reply arrived several minutes after the initial email was

sent. No one at the FBI office expected such a quick response, but in minutes Franc Liebmann received a reply from Kate.

FLiebmann

Tomorrow, 2pm, Café Utrecht in old Utrecht. I will be traveling from Amsterdam on the 1pm train. I will meet you there. After the money is wired into my account, Belize Islands Bank #88334090, I will give you the information and items I have.

Kate Williams

KWilliams

The decision to communicate to Franc Liebmann that Kate would arrive by train from Amsterdam alarmed both Jake and Kate, but once Agent Porter explained in order to show Liebmann that this was an amateurish plan, they relaxed and agreed to the arrangement. Agent Porter's hoped to draw out the other participants of Liebmann's project, primarily Dieter Brach and Brit Vanheijsen. Agent Porter assured Kate that she would be safe and surrounded at all times by undercover police and FBI agents.

The Utrecht café that Jake and Kate had visited turned out to be an excellent place for the exchange. Undercover officers would be in place, ready and waiting for the 2pm meeting tomorrow. The afternoon meeting meant they could meet during a quieter time of the day, allowing agents to get into position. Jake and Agent Porter would travel by car to Utrecht and be available when needed for the exchange. Kate would travel by train with three undercover agents. As soon as Kate began the meeting with Liebmann, she would show a video on her laptop of the vial and the information sent to her by Buck. Once the money was wired into the account, Jake would show up with copies of the documents and the cell vial. Once the exchange took place, Franc Liebmann would be apprehended and taken into custody.

The next morning came quickly for Jake and Kate who were nervously anticipating the task that awaited them. Paul Baker called early that morning and assured them he was aware of the plan and he felt comfortable that appropriate measures had been taken to make sure they would be safe. Paul's call helped calm them down a bit but still they knew that what they faced was very dangerous. They knew first hand just what these people were capable of doing.

After a good breakfast at their hotel in The Hague, Jake and Kate went downstairs to wait in the lobby for Agent Porter. Sitting on a couch facing the front door at the far end of the lobby, they both stared forward without saying a word.

Jake broke the silence, "Kate you can back out now. You don't have to do this."

"I have to. My job, your practice, and Buck's death…these people need to be stopped."

"Okay then, once we get through this, I promise we will take some time together to wind down and make sense of all this. Our relationship has so much promise and has moved along so fast, but we both have to admit that although the events of the last couple of weeks brought us together, it's time to move on to the next phase of our relationship."

Kate leaned over and gave Jake a kiss on the cheek. "Now that is a promise I will hold you to."

Before Jake could respond, Agent Porter appeared at the front door of the lobby. "You guys ready for an adventure?"

They both stood up, shrugged their shoulders and walked toward Agent Porter.

"As ready as I'll ever be," Kate answered.

"Let's do this before I chicken out," Jake added.

"Okay, let's go." Agent Porter turned and led Jake and Kate out the door to a waiting car.

The drive to the Central Station in Amsterdam took about an hour. During the trip Agent Porter reviewed the plan repeatedly, until he was sure everyone knew every detail. Kate would soon be dropped off to join the three undercover agents for the train trip to Utrecht, then Jake and Agent Porter would drive to Utrecht to join the rest of the team already in place. Jake and Agent Porter would arrive in Utrecht before the train since they were actually leaving about an hour before the train.

As they approached the train station, Kate's hand tightened around Jake's. Sensing her anxiety he slid closer to her and whispered the words, "It'll be okay. I promise." As soon as the car stopped, Kate got out and the three agents traveling with her walked up near the car to join her. Jake slid out behind her to say goodbye with a protective hug and kiss.

"I'll see you soon. Be careful and remember that I love you." He was surprised that the words had fallen out of his mouth so easily. It just happened and he had said it. From almost that first instant on the plane he knew he was in love with her but he was cautious, scared of his feelings, and of course he didn't want to frighten her off.

Surprised and delighted to hear his words Kate answered, "Jake, I promise I'll be careful. And....I love you too. I have since that first flight over here. So don't worry about me, I wouldn't dare miss the rest of our lives together." With that she hugged and kissed him again and turned to join the three agents.

The train ride began uneventfully. Kate sat in a second class car as Jake had taught her on her first trip to The Netherlands. She tried to relax and enjoy the Dutch countryside but she found herself checking constantly for the three agents riding with her. Each agent randomly sat throughout the car, blending in well with the rest of the passengers in the car. She felt safe knowing her protectors were nearby. When the train was traveling between stations, Kate relaxed and enjoyed the ride and scenery, but each time it pulled into a station, the nervousness returned and Kate became uneasy about the mission that lay ahead. Oh how she wished they had taken the non-stop train to Utrecht.

The last stop before they arrived in Utrecht seemed no different at first. The train pulled into the station and the platform filled with people getting on and off the train. Kate nervously checked out each person exiting and boarding the train as she waited anxiously until it closed the doors and started to move. Then she saw him, the man from the accident, the man who gave the briefing in Triumph, Dieter something. What is he doing here on the train? Is he looking for me?

The train pulled out of the station. Scared, she didn't look up for several minutes. Dieter Brach, seated two rows away, locked eyes with her. He nodded, his gaze narrow and probing. She felt trapped and forced herself to break eye contact. This was the worst possible thing that could happen. All too quickly her mind flew back to when she first saw him at Lansdun after Buck's murder. Now, he was only feet away, watching her. Would this trip ever be over? She fought the panic rising, the urge to look around and see if the agents had spotted him. She looked out the window to avoid his stare and told herself to breathe.

The last ten minutes of the train ride seemed like it would never end. As the train pulled into the Utrecht station, Kate took advantage of the crowd and exited out the opposite end of the car from Dieter, allowing herself to get ahead of him by mingling her way through the crowd. She hurried downstairs to the main area of the station and found the women's restroom. Fumbling for some change, she paid the attendant and disappeared inside. After washing her face with a cold cloth and touching up her makeup, Kate felt calm enough to leave the safety of the restroom. She headed out into the main corridor of the station and noticed each of the agents waiting in the background. With confidence, she moved out of the terminal into the street where she looked to hail a cab that would take her to the café in old Utrecht. At the taxi stand, she waited until it was her turn. The man attending to the cab traffic had just acknowledged it was her turn next, when a black Mercedes pulled in front of the next cab in line. The back door opened and before she knew it, Dieter Brach pushed her into the back seat, slid in behind her, and slammed the door. She recognized the man on the other side of her from her time at Lansdun headquarters as Franc Liebmann. Brit Vanheijsen drove. The car sped out of the station as Kate sat in horror of her new predicament.

It happened so quickly. The three agents were only footsteps away but could do nothing to prevent her abduction. The lead agent immediately notified Agent Porter and after flashing badges, jumped into the next cab that sped out of the station to follow Kate and her Utrecht hosts.

"Good Morning, Ms. Williams, I am Franc Liebmann. I believe we met several weeks ago during the quarterly meeting at Lansdun Headquarters. I believe you have already met Dieter Brach and Brit Vanheijsen. I thought it would be in my best interest to pick you up today and deal with the little problem you brought to my attention in your email. I hope you have what I am looking for. I've arranged another place for our meeting, just in case you involved the police in our little exchange.

The drive lasted only for a few moments and Kate recognized their destination. The car had stopped in front of the office of Jan Metler, Tandarts, the same office that Jake had shown her on their visit to Utrecht a week earlier. The back door of the car opened and Franc Liebmann and Dieter Brach hastily escorted Kate into the office. Her heart pounded, but she knew better than to struggle, knowing what could happen if she angered these men. Her only hope was that the undercover agents were able to follow her.

"May I help you?" a young woman politely asked as the group walked into the small reception room of the office. Then she recognized Franc Liebmann and said, "Oh Mr. Liebmann I did not see you at first. Dr. Metler is with a patient. I will tell him you are here."

"No Margit, we will wait in his office. Dismiss his patient and tell him to come quick now," Liebmann demanded.

Margit thought about arguing but the cold look in Mr. Liebmann eyes and the stare she received from the man with him gave her an eerie chill. She felt it best to do what these men wanted. She opened the door of the inner office and directed them to Dr. Metler's large oak paneled office with floor to ceiling bookcases on every wall .Once inside, Dieter ordered Kate to a chair by a table in the corner and stood watch by the door. Franc Liebmann sat in the chair next to Kate.

Just then the door opened and Dr. Metler came rushing in. "Franc, just what is the meaning of this barging into my office uninvited? I have a patient here." No sooner had he finished than he noticed Dieter Brach standing guard by the doorway. The menacing look Dieter gave him was enough for him to change his demeanor.

"Jan, get rid of your patient and send Margit home. We need the office. You will need to stay here. Do it now"

Jan Metler walked over to the desk and paged Margit. "Margit would you please dismiss Bergit, she is all finished. You can go as well. I have some business here with Franc Liebmann."

"Yes sir, Dr. Metler. I will lock the door on my way out, Ja?" Margit replied.

"Yes, thank you." Jan Metler hung up the phone and sat behind his desk facing Franc Liebmann.

Just as Margit exited the office and turned to lock the front door, the agents following the black Mercedes pulled up. One of the agents, a Dutch policewoman, got out of the car and approached Margit. Showing her KMar ID badge to Margit, she grabbed her by the arm and escorted her over to the car.

"We believe two men took the woman in this picture into the office you just left . Have you seen her?"

Margit hesitated. "I won't betray Dr. Metler." She looked down at her hands clutched in her lap. "Is he in trouble?" She looked up at the policewoman, then quickly back at her fingers winding in and out of each other. Finally, she raised her head, eyes closed, and whispered, "Yes I believe that woman just went inside. Is there some kind of trouble?"

Ignoring the question, the Dutch policewoman held up two photographs. "What about these men? Was she with them?"

Margit's face paled. "Yes. She was with Franc Liebmann and this man." She pointed at the picture of Brach. "They are with Dr. Metler now in his office."

"Is the lady okay?"

"Yes, she seemed fine. Maybe a little nervous, but fine."

"Thank you. We will need you to give us some more information. This officer will ask you some questions. Please get into the car."

The events that occurred at the train station were not exactly as Agent Porter had planned but he was glad that he had planted the GPS tracking device into the lining of Kate's briefcase. The suspense of Kate's kidnapping lasted only a few minutes when it was discovered the cars had stopped a few blocks from the café. The agents mobilized and surrounded the dentist's office.

Jake saw the commotion and sensed something was not right. About 30 minutes before Agent Porter told him that Kate had arrived at the station and would be coming to the café across the street very soon. Surely she should have been here by now he thought. He approached Agent Porter who was conferring with several agents and officers from the Dutch police force. "Agent Porter, what's going on? I saw all the agents get in a car and leave. Where were they going? Where is Kate?" Jake asked, feeling panic rise.

Agent Porter excused himself and turned to Jake. He pointed to a chair and sat down with Jake. "There has been a small glitch in our plans. Kate was forced into a car at the train station. Our agents just informed me that Dieter Brach was on the train. The briefcase she carried has a GPS tracking device in it and we know where she is: a dental office several blocks away from here. We just questioned someone who works there. Kate is inside the dental office and the lady said she is okay."

"Metler, right? Jake replied, "The dentist."

"Yeah Metler, Jan Metler. Isn't that the guy you think--"

"Yeah, that is the guy who placed the cell samples in the teeth. I can almost guarantee you she is there with Franc Liebmann and Dieter Brach. So what are you doing now? Kate could be, no, she is in real danger. You need to get her out of there."

"Hold on Jake. We have the place under surveillance. No one has left or entered the Metler's office since Kate arrived. I am sure Kate will be contacting you soon."

Franc Liebmann abruptly stood. "Ms. Williams, I believe you have something for me."

"I do, but you have changed the plans. You pushed me into a car and brought me here under protest."

"Well, as long as you get your money I don't think it matters where we meet. This suited my needs much better. Besides we now have a more private venue to conduct our business. Show me what you have for me."

"Mr. Liebmann, I was concerned something like this would happen so I will only supply the material you want once the money is wired into the Belize Bank account I sent you. I have a live video of the vial and the material you wanted that Buck McFadden sent me. Why don't you let me show you what I have."

"Well, Ms. Williams, this certainly is a surprise. Of course I have someone at my bank ready to wire the money, but I guess I have no choice but to let you show me your video."

Kate opened up her briefcase and turned on her laptop and within seconds the video link was cued up to Franc Liebmann, Dr. Metler , and Dieter Brach. The video opened with Jake Patterson sitting at a table. Jake began to speak.

"Mr. Liebmann, my name is Dr. Jake Patterson and I am a dentist in Triumph, Texas. In fact I am the dentist with the office that I believe one of your colleagues set fire to and left a body inside to burn. Ms. Williams and I have managed to rescue the cell sample that you had smuggled into our country inside a crown covered molar. Upon removing the tooth of your last courier, Willem Voorhis, I discovered the glass vial with the crown. The plan might have worked if the root canals had been done properly." Franc Liebmann gave Jan Metler a look of disgust forcing Dr. Metler to respond with a shrug of the shoulders. "I then had the vial examined by a laboratory technician and placed in a protective incubator to keep it viable. Here you can see the incubator and you can see the vial is inside the container. I also have a collection of documents that Kate received from Buck McFadden after his death that I am sure you also want. I am close by and will give the documents and the cell vial to Dr. Jan Metler only after the money has been wired into our account."

The video showed Jake dialing a phone and within seconds Kate's phone rang from her briefcase.

Franc Liebmann directed Kate to give him her cell phone.

"Mr. Liebmann, I am waiting for the money to be wired into our account. As soon as it is, I ask that Dr. Metler meet me, along with Kate. When the money is wired I will call back on this phone."

Franc stood up and moved across the room to where Jan Metler was seated. He called Dieter over and the three of them discussed what the next move would be. The room was small and Kate could hear them talking. Franc wanted it over. Jan Metler wanted out as well. Only Dieter felt it dangerous to let Kate walk out. He considered Kate and Dr. Patterson liabilities. They seemed to agree the money would be wired, when Franc looked up and noticed Kate watching. He pushed the group farther into the corner and began to whisper. Franc Liebmann picked up his phone and called his man at the bank.

Moments later Jake saw on his computer screen that the 3 million Euros had been wired into the account. Now it was his turn to do his part of the deal. He dialed Kate's number. The phone was answered by Franc Liebmann. Jake spoke first. "Mr. Liebmann, send Dr. Metler to the apothecary shop on the corner. I will meet him there with the cell vial and the material you need. He must bring Kate with him."

"Fine, I will do this."

Dr. Metler and Kate exited cautiously out the front door of the office and walked down the street to the front of the apothecary shop. They opened the door and went inside, where they were greeted by several FBI agents. A shocked Dr. Metler was immediately taken into custody. Kate looked toward the back of the shop and found Jake standing up against the back counter.

"Kate, are you all right?"

Kate ran to Jake and almost knocked him over with a hug and a kiss. They held each other for several seconds, neither one saying a word. Kate broke the silence.

"I'm all right now. I have to admit I was pretty scared. You would have been proud of me. I really kept my cool the whole time, but I don't think I want to make this my full time job."

"I thought I had lost you when you got hauled off in that car. I'm so glad this is over."

Looking outside the shop, Kate and Jake could see Franc Liebmann and Dieter Brach being taken away in handcuffs. Agent Porter walked over to them.

"It seems that Dieter bolted out the back door of the office so he could meet up with you guys after the transaction. Thank goodness the

KMar were there waiting. Then it was just a matter of minutes before the officers entered the office and arrested Franc Liebmann. Brit Vanheijsen was arrested earlier shortly after dropping off Kate, Liebmann, and Dieter Brach at Metler's office. Oh, by the way, I just got off the phone with Chief Baker and he told me they are going to arrest Dr. Jamison now. They didn't want anybody tipping him off earlier. He also wanted me to tell you that he's glad you are both safe."

With his arm firmly around Kate's shoulder, Jake took a deep breath. "Agent Porter, the last couple of hours were pretty harrowing. I can't remember ever being that scared, I am so glad this is over."

"Yeah, for a minute there, even I thought I might have lost Kate. All is well now. This chain of events is finally over."

"Folks, I don't think this would have been solved so fast without your help. Your government and the Dutch government are extremely grateful for your help. It's time for us all to head back to The Hague for some much needed rest. We need you one more day for a debriefing then you are free to spend as much time here as you'd like before you fly home. The cars will be here in a minute, and then we can head on back to The Hague."

"Agent Porter, I hope you won't mind if Kate and I are go back by train. We have a lot to talk about. We'll catch up with you tomorrow. What time do we need to be at the FBI office?

"How about 9 am?"

"We'll be there." Jake and Kate turned and walked hand in hand down the cobblestone road as they headed to the train station.

"Jake, you know how you always said we should travel second class on the train?"

"Yeah, I remember. People watching!"

"Well tonight we are riding first class. No more second class for us. I have had just about enough people watching for one day," she said with a broad smile.

Jake laughed, "I bet you have. Come on, maybe we can catch the next train." They quickened their pace and hurried the rest of the way to the train station.

Chapter 26

Kate and Jake's world had changed when the sun came up the next day. The sun looked brighter and there was not a cloud in the sky. Very unusual weather for The Netherlands but it was a perfect way to start a new life together. They began the morning by taking a walk around the hotel. The sun was shining but the air was still cool and brisk. As they walked down the almost empty streets they were passed by bicycle commuters or an occasional car making its way to work. Soon they came upon a small outdoor café and decided to stop for breakfast. As they sat down a waiter approached and asked in Dutch if they would care to read the morning paper. Jake answered yes and then they both ordered coffee and breakfast.

As soon as the paper arrived Jake looked at the front page and saw that their story had made the news. The headline read "Corporate Espionage Plot Solved" and right next to it in an adjoining story was the announcement that Willem Van Hollenvat, son of Rijkaard Van Hollenvat, CEO of Lansdun International had been found alive and well after being missing for several days. The story spoke of how help from the FBI and the KMar along with two individuals from the little town of Triumph, Texas, were instrumental in solving the mystery of his disappearance. Then there in the next paragraph in bold print were their names and pictures. With that newspaper article little did they know that they would be thrust into several weeks of notoriety and fame.

Kate and Jake made their way back to the hotel and waited to be picked up by Agent Porter for their debriefing.

The debriefing went as planned with no surprises. Agent Porter and his colleagues reviewed every detail of the case, Kate and Jake spent several hours being interviewed, and finally the mystery of the crown deception was put to rest. Toward the end of the session, Peter Hart appeared and asked to speak with Kate and Jake before they left. After thanking them on behalf of the Van Hollenvat family for their help in solving the disappearance of Willem, he handed them each a small envelope labeled with their names written in ornate calligraphy. Inside each envelope they found an engraved invitation written in Dutch, from Rijkaard Van Hollenvat inviting them to a reception in their honor. Mr. Hart also invited any of Jake's family here in The Netherlands. Jake couldn't wait to tell his grandparents of the special invitation. He knew his Oma would be thrilled.

After spending the night with his Oma and Opa, Jake and Kate woke up to the busy preparations for the trip that evening to visit Lansdun International's headquarters. Oma and Opa beamed with pride after learning that Jake and his new friend would be honored at the reception. Oma found their best outfits and cleaned and pressed them to make them perfect for the event.

Jake and Kate went into town that afternoon to buy clothing appropriate for the party. The hustle and bustle around the Leiden Hotel couldn't have been at a higher level unless the Queen had been coming to lunch. Oma insisted that everyone look perfect before they were picked up.

"Oma, you can't tease me anymore about me wanting to get somewhere on time. You have out staged me today."

"Jakob, you should treat your Oma nicer than that. Today is a very special day. I am going to a reception in my Grandson's honor. I have the right to want everything perfect."

"I'm just teasing you. You are the best Oma a guy could ever have and I do love you."

"I love you too, my little Jakob. Thank you for this day." She stood on her tiptoes and gave him a big hug and kiss. Jake could not remember when she had been more excited about anything.

Almost as soon as everyone was ready, there was a knock on the door. Opa got up and opened the door to find a man in a suit.

"Hello, I am Peter Hart. I am here to pick you up for your special day. Is everyone ready?"

"It's nice to meet you Mr. Hart. My wife and I have heard so much about you. We are ready. Let me tell the others you are here."

"Mr. Hart?" Kate said, surprised. "You are picking us up?"

"Yes Kate. I am your escort until you leave the country."

The reception was filled with the usual fanfare one might expect from an audience with a head of state rather than the owner of a large company. Willem greeted Jake's family at the door and escorted them to meet his parents. Willem's parents graciously thanked them both and offered them any Lansdun resource for the length of their stay in The Netherlands.

On the way back home, Oma could do nothing but continue to repeat how proud she was of her wonderful grandson. It truly was a special event in her life. Although Jake and Kate wouldn't want to have to go through it all again, they were glad Oma was touched the way she had been.

Over the next few weeks, Jake took Kate to all of his favorite places in the country that he loved. Everywhere they went, they were instantly recognized as the two Americans on the front page of the paper who had helped solve the Van Hollenvat disappearance. They were given access to the best tables at restaurants, free passes into tourist attractions, and a general respect from everyone they met while in the country. Yet soon it was time to start back to Triumph and try to make sense of their lives.

Agent Porter, who they both now considered a friend, drove them to the airport. They had said their goodbyes earlier to Oma and Opa and the little town of Leiden, but now it was time to say goodbye to The Netherlands and head back home.

"I can't thank you enough. Without your help I am sure this case would still be a mystery. By the way, the three million Euros is for you to keep. I just got word this morning from Mr. Van Hollenvat. Good Luck with everything guys. I really think we made a good team. You never know when I might need you guys again."

Jake laughed. "Yeah I'm sure that won't be anytime soon. A small town dentist and a biotechnology executive fighting crime across the world just doesn't seem like the makings of the next crime fighting team."

Kate looked at Jake with surprise, "Hey, speak for yourself, I thought I did pretty good. I guess you will have to be my junior partner."

The long flight home was smooth but welcomed since both Jake and Kate were ready for some relaxation from the craziness of the last four weeks. As they left the baggage claim area at the Houston Airport, they discovered their involvement in the case was news back home. Lauren and her husband, the twins, Chief Baker, Jake's staff and what seemed to be the rest of Triumph, Texas, waited for them. They'd barely begun to hug and say hi to everyone when a swarm of reporters stuck microphones in their faces and began asking a barrage of questions. Chief Baker quickly took charge of the situation and informed everyone that there would be a press conference held the next day at the Triumph Police Station. He then proceeded to escort Jake and Kate to a car waiting to hurry them away to their homes in Triumph.

Family and friends gathered for the next several hours at Jake's house. Lauren had organized a reception with the help of Jake's staff. Everyone in town seemed to be there to congratulate and talk with Jake and Kate. Finally as the night grew late, Lauren dismissed the guests and began the task of cleaning up after the party. The twins were already put to bed in one of the guest rooms. Kate fell quickly asleep and as Jake got ready for bed he heard Lauren still cleaning up downstairs.

He headed back down to the living room. "Lauren, this can wait until tomorrow. Why don't you go to bed?"

"You're the one who should be in bed. You have that press conference tomorrow."

"I got some sleep on the plane. Kate was exhausted, though; she couldn't stay up any longer."

"How are you doing? Have you thought about what you're going to do now?"

"Kate and I are thinking about taking some time off. She's never been to Belize."

"That sounds like a great idea. I can call Mr. Slim and Susan and tell them you're coming, as soon as you have some firm plans."

The press conference the next day threatened to turn into a zoo, but Chief Baker handled it like a pro. Jake and Kate answered questions after Chief Baker made a statement concerning the basic facts of the case. It lasted almost an hour, much too long for the jetlagged Jake and Kate. Over the next few days their pictures were in newspapers and on local Houston television, but soon their story faded away, like so many stories on the evening news.

Jake finally received the insurance settlement on his dental practice, but since returning from Europe he had decided not to open his practice again. He visited with each staff member to thank them for their loyalty over the years and gave each a sizable bonus to help out until they found another job. Once things settled down, he contacted several dentists in Triumph about taking over his patient base.

The morning after the press conference, Kate visited with Greg Wilson, who encouraged her to take some time off before coming back to work.

"Kate, I feel like I work with a real super hero. I've arranged for you to take as much time as you need with pay. What you did for Lansdun International ultimately saved us millions of dollars. Headquarters wants you to take as much time as you need. Just send post cards when you can."

When she arrived back at Jake's, he opened her car door and gave her a big hug. "Kate, I really missed you."

"I've only been gone for about an hour."

"What I mean is I really have missed spending time with you alone. The last few days I've had to share you with the world."

"Well, I am a famous crime fighter now. You may just have to wait your turn." She smiled and leaned in for a kiss, which Jake met eagerly.

"Kate, Let's get away, spend some time together and build on this great start we have had. I thought we'd go to Belize. What do you think?"

Chapter 27

The intense morning sunshine upon the front porch signaled the beginning of a new day, but that was okay with Kate. Since arriving in Belize she had finally gotten the rest she had desperately needed over the last weeks. The house on the beach with it's incredible views was just how Jake had described it. From her Vantage point in a chaise lounge, Kate looked off the deck to the sandy beach beyond that separated the deck and the water by only about 75 feet. From the edge of the water a long pier shot out into the ocean about another 100 feet ending in a 10 x 10 square platform covered by a thatched roof palapa. There one could fish or relax, safely protected from the hot Belizean sun. The water seemed to go endlessly toward the eastern horizon, only disturbed by a white ripple showing where the reef broke the waves into a calm progression toward the shore. The blue green color of the water reflected the colors in the blue sky above. Today there were a few clouds accenting the sky, waiting to be filled with rain for the routine afternoon showers that go away as quickly as they come. Paradise, Kate thought, simply paradise. They had only been there two days but the relaxing Belizean atmosphere was the therapy that Kate truly needed.

The flight from Houston had arrived at Belize International airport in the middle of the afternoon on a bright sunny day and after easily processing through customs and immigration. Jake and Kate had made their way to the domestic terminal to await the flight to San Pedro on Ambergris Caye. The word easy was an understatement. They had walked off the plane with all the other passengers and proceeded to get in the Custom and Immigration line labeled Non Residents. No sooner had they stopped than Jake was tapped on the shoulder by a Customs official. Kate thought to herself, oh no not again, thinking that they were being stopped by the local police. She had had just about enough of the cops and robbers thing. Quickly she was put at ease when the tall black man grabbed Jake and pulled him into a big hug.

"Docta Jake, welcome back home. You are in the wrong line. Come bring your lady friend we need to get you out to San Pedro." The man turned and returned to his desk at the end of the Resident Line and waived them both over.

Jake grabbed his bag and signaled Kate to follow as they moved to the head of the Resident Line to stand before the man seated on a barstool high chair behind the Customs desk. Jake turned to Kate and said, "Kate, this is my good friend Gusto. We've spent a lot of time together during the last 10 years. Gusto, this is Kate."

"Finally, Docta Jake has a lady friend. You got a special man Miss Kate."

"Thank you. I think so. too." She smiled.

"Docta Jake give me those passports. He stamped the passports and gave them both back to Jake. I bet you have a plane to catch to San Pedro. I went by the house while fishing the other day. It is looking great. Oh, I almost forgot." He said with a twinkle in his eye, "How is Miss Lauren? Is she coming down too?"

Jake laughed, "Gusto, you never have gotten over that crush you used to have, have you? You sly dog. You better not let your wife hear you talk that way."

Gusto turned red as an apple even through his dark skin. "Oh Docta Jake, you cannot tell Miss Yoli."

"Don't worry man. Your secret is safe. Now you must come out to the house to see us. We will be here awhile."

"No problem! Docta Jake. No problem!"

Jake and Kate moved through the line and walked the 20 steps to the baggage retrieval area. There neatly placed were all their bags. Standing beside them was a thin Mayan looking man.

"Docta Jake!" he called out. "I have your bags. I knew by the Green and Gold ribbon that they had to be yours. I already talked to the immigration guy. We are cleared to leave. Let's go!"

"As always Hector, you make it so easy to get into the country."

"Yes sir, Docta Jake. Anything for you and Miss Lauren. How are the twins?"

"They are growing up real fast."

"Docta Jake, who ya lady friend?" He spoke with a thick Belizean Creole.

"Hector, this is Kate."

"Nice to meet you Kate. Welcome to Belize."

"Nice to meet you too Hector. Thank you. I already feel very welcome here."

"Docta Jake, Tropic Air right?"

"Right as usual Hector. Thanks."

Jake tipped Hector well as he always did and he grabbed all the bags and moved through two doors into the departure terminal.

The couple then walked through the last Immigration obstacle and proceeded through doors into the main lobby of the airport. Once inside, Kate was amazed at how each of the small ticket counters were all so busy.

The flight out to Ambergris Caye to the San Pedro Airport was something out of the movies. The small twin engine Otter lifted off the runway and glided gracefully into a turn to head northeast across the water for the 20 minute flight. This day was cloudy, the white fluffy kind that almost look like cotton candy. The views out of the plane were spectacular. The white jagged line of waves breaking over the reef clearly showed the protective barrier the reef provided for the outer Cayes.

After they landed and made their way out of the plane, they waited outside in the heat for their bags to be unloaded from the plane. Just as Jake had collected all their bags, he turned to Kate and said, "Welcome to San Pedro! Our home away from home."

"What happens now?" Kate asked as she surveyed the busy activity on the street in front of the tiny airport terminal. The airport was located within walking distance of center of San Pedro.

Just then a voice called out from a golf cart that had just pulled up in the sandy street. "Mista Jake. Over here!"

"Kate, here's our ride. Help me with the bags please."

They walked over to the golf cart where an elderly couple waited.

"Kate, this is Mr. Slim and his wife Susan, they're caretakers at our house here. You met their son Gusto at the airport. They have come to take us to the house. Mr. Slim, Miss Susan, this is Kate, who I spoke about when I called you to tell you we were coming."

Mr. Slim, a tall black Creole man, reached out and shook Kate's hand and responded in a gentle voice, "Ah Miss Kate, Jake spoke about you like he was a school boy. It is so good to see some joy back in his life. Welcome to San Pedro. I hope you consider it your home."

Miss Susan spoke, "Kate, welcome home. I have been cooking all day and we are going to have Jake's favorite for supper tonight."

Mr. Slim climbed slowly out of the golf cart to help Jake with the bags. Jake stopped him and said, "Mr. Slim, I can handle this. It is okay. How are the both of you?"

Miss Susan answered in a soft but polite voice, "Oh, Jake we are just grand. Getting a little older but doing grand. It is so good to see you."

Kate and Jake climbed into the golf cart and Mr. Slim drove the short distance to a boat dock in the center of town. There waiting for them was an open boat with a center console with the name "Triumph" painted across the back. Mr. Slim helped Miss Susan and Kate into the boat while Jake attended to the luggage.

"Jake, you take the ladies to the house and I will be there soon. I have some errands to do. Gusto called and he is coming over later. We will get a ride on the water taxi." Mr. Slim turned and walked back toward town.

Jake climbed into the boat where Kate and Miss Susan waited, then fired up the engine and moved the boat slowly away from the dock. Once he cleared the dock past the more congested area, he opened up the throttle and cruised smoothly north toward his house. The boat ride was an easy 5 mile trip that lasted about 20 minutes. Along the way Kate was educated on the history of San Pedro and how much it had changed since Jake and Lauren first started coming there many years ago. They passed a few isolated fisherman, snorkeling expeditions, and boats returning from a day of scuba diving. Soon Jake slowed the boat and veered in toward the shore to a house that would be home for the next several weeks.

Not sure if Kate was asleep or awake on the porch, Jake whispered in her ear, "Kate, Kate are you awake?" The bright sun made it hard for him to see through the sunglasses to know whether her eyes were open.

"Yeah, just a little daydream. I was just thinking about how much I'm enjoying Belize. Jake, I know I have said this to you many times since we got here, but this place is so perfect, so peaceful."

"It sure is." And with that comment Jake climbed onto the lounge chair next to Kate and laid back to enjoy the morning sun.

A water taxi approached and Jake stood up to get a better glimpse of their visitor. He began his way down the pier and got to the palapa covered deck just as the water taxi approached.

"Hello Mista Jake," said the boat driver, "I brought you a visitor."

As the boat pulled up, a man dressed in a light seersucker suit with a tie, climbed awkwardly out of the boat. He looked extremely out of place and seemed somewhat uncomfortable with the already hot day. When he stood up fully, he seemed to regain some of his composure.

"Are you Jake Patterson?" Without waiting for an answer he proceeded, "It took me awhile to track you people down. I am actually looking for Kate Williams."

Somewhat suspicious and feeling protective, Jake asked, "I'm sorry I didn't catch your name and why do you need to see Kate Williams?"

"Oh I am sorry. My name is John Granger and I am from New England Fidelity Insurance. I'm here to settle a claim. Here is my company card and passport."

"What kind of claim?" Jake prodded for more information before allowing Mr. Granger to approach his house.

"Well, under normal circumstances I would only talk with Ms. Williams, but considering the trouble I have had in finding her I guess it won't hurt to tell you." He put his briefcase down, opened it, and pulled out a piece of paper, handing it to Jake. "Buck McFadden, who I believe was a friend of Ms. Williams, named her as beneficiary on his life insurance policy."

After scanning the document, Jake invited Mr. Granger to come up and talk to Kate at the house. Before making the walk, Mr. Granger asked the taxi driver to wait for him and that he would only be a few moments. Once up at the house Mr. Granger explained to Kate that Buck McFadden had taken out an insurance policy with Kate Williams as the beneficiary. Once he affirmed her identity and had her sign a form, he handed her an envelope, turned and left almost as quickly as he arrived.

To Kate's surprise, inside the envelope was a hand-written letter from Buck and a cashier's check for three million dollars. She opened the letter and read:

Dear Kate,

If you are reading this letter you have just been surprised with the settlement from the insurance company. As you might remember I have no living family. Since we began our friendship back in New Jersey you have been the only person I could really call family. During our friendship you always treated me with respect and took the time to listen. You were always there when I needed you. Don't ever underestimate the impact of kind words and a listening ear.

Thank you for the joy you have brought to my life.

Your friend,

Buck McFadden

Kate put the letter down and wiped the tears from her eyes. When she looked at the check the tears turned into sobbing. The events of the last few weeks finally were over and now she allowed herself to mourn her friend's death. Jake sat down next to her on the lounge chair and held her close as she finally was able to cry it out. He listened as she told him about her friendship with Buck and as she retraced the days leading up to his death. After a few minutes, she asked to be left alone, so Jake went inside. Later, he looked outside and could see her staring off into the eastern sky.

Jake soon fell asleep on the couch and was awakened with a gentle kiss on the lips. Kate snuggled in next to him and spoke softly.

"Jake, sweetie, I'm back. I'm okay now."

"Are you sure you're alright?"

"Yeah, thanks for letting me cry. I needed to do that."

"I figured you deserve a good cry." With a grin he exclaimed, "Besides it gave me a chance to take a nap."

"So now what do we do? Where do we go from here? "

"All I know is that I am with you and I am not letting you out of my sight. I suppose we can relax here for a while but you told Greg you were going back to work in a couple of weeks."

Kate held up the check from the insurance company and waved it in front of Jake and said, "I am not so sure I want to do that, but I guess I don't need to really decide that today do I?"

He looked at her with loving eyes and asked, "Kate, have I told you that I love you today?"

She coyly answered, "Only about 10 times. But you are going to have to do way better than that."

Jake stood up and grabbed her hand, leading her to the bedroom, "Well I think I know a good way to work on that."

Just then Jake's cell phone rang. Without hesitation he answered the phone, recognizing the number. "Hi Paul.".

"Jake, sorry to bother you but Agent Porter and I have something we think you and Kate can help us with," Paul said in an almost apologetic tone.

Kate stood across from Jake with her arms crossed with a smile on her face and asked, "Is that Paul?"

Jake nodded yes to Kate as he listened to Paul.

Kate reached over and grabbed the phone from Jake and spoke to Paul. "Paul, this is Kate. Jake will call you later, he is busy right now," she said as she smiled at Jake. "He will call you back later."

Paul attempted to speak to Kate but before he could get out a word Kate hung up the phone and turned it off.

"Now where were we?" Kate threw the cell phone down on the couch, took Jake's hand and pulled him toward the back room. Jake did not resist.

CPSIA information can be obtained at www.ICGtesting.com
Printed in the USA
LVOW060148110112

263176LV00001B/12/P